The Day Xyron Fell

By: Erin McMillan

Acknowledgments

My mom: Victoria D. McMillan

My boyfriend: Carlos Barraza

My friends: Keiko, Ashley, Gretel

My Teachers: Mrs. Dipeppe (English teacher) & Mr. Carter (Art teacher)

and of course you. The very thoughtful person who picked up my book and decided to give it a chance. A special thanks to all of you. This book wouldn't be possible without you.

"This is how you do it: You sit down at the keyboard and you put one word after another until it's done. It's that easy, and that hard."

- Neil Gaiman

Author Signature

This book is intended for

ages 17 and up

<u>Prologue</u>

Year 2403

"Come on children gather around. It's story time." dad calls.

My sisters, brothers, and I gather around the fire. It's dark outside even for La Bobo Cree. The fire crackles and the stars twinkle in the night sky. We're all sitting in a semi-circle waiting for my dad Vance to tell us our bedtime story for the night. Warm sand sliding and settling between our toes. Our knees in front of us touching our chest. Arms wrapped around them. Some of us so excited that we rock back and forth.

"What story should I tell tonight?" he says to himself.

We are all on the edge of our seats. Dying for him to start the tale of the night. What 6 year old doesn't love their parents' stories? Especially since my dad tells the best stories. Sometimes he even tells us folktales. Which is what I prefer. Cause even though it's only what people say and pass on. I know there's a small grain of truth somewhere in there. Under all the shock factor and the happy ever after. There's definitely some truth to it. There has to be. I hope tonight he tells us one like that. Not the kind where he makes it up as he goes along.

"Yara, pay attention. I'm about to start." my dad says to me.

"Yes, sir."

"Tonight will be a famous folktale among everyone in Xyron. A story that was told to me when I was your age."

We all giggle at the thought. Not being able to imagine my dad being so young.

He continues "Long ago, There was an unnamed hero. It was said that he broke into what was known as the inner circle of hell in their day and age. The hero's goal was to save the people. From disaster and from poverty. To create a more homely and more welcoming place among the people. Where everyone was equal. This was unheard of and far fetched. Everyone thought it was insanity. Not even possible. It sounds silly, even to me after all this time. But that's not the point. Anyway, our unnamed hero trekked across the land. One day, deciding that everything would be easier if Hell was just extinguished from the inside out. Hell's foundation needed to be broken. Remind you our unnamed hero was completely crazy. So he somehow convinced himself that the only way to save the people of our land, was to flood all the core buildings. Continuously sneaking into the chambers of the most sacred buildings and flooding them with water. Of course, no one knows where he got all this water. But one day it is said that after flooding the main buildings of all 5 regions of the mainland. Peace actually fell upon the land. Everyone believed that it had something to do with the last flood being on an eclipse. Or maybe it was the fact that he destroyed so much stuff from the flood. That the people needed to work together to restore all that was lost from what little they had, to begin with."

"That sounds so cool." the words slipping out of my mouth without warning.

"Yes, it was. An what he did worked. People said that there was peace for many years. But as the people got older, everyone eventually died off. Or just stopped believing that such a thing was possible. If anyone did openly admit that they believed in this being possible outside of being some tall tale. It was a sign of weakness. How could one rely on such a thing for world peace? But in the hearts of many people throughout the land. Secretly, people are waiting for another unnamed hero like that to rise again. And save our people."

‡   ‡   ‡

<u>Chapter 1</u>

Year 2904

The air is dry, bitter, and still. I slightly dig my nails into the red brick wall but I stop due to the fact it crumbles away. Leaving red dust in my palm, and little chips under my nails. How distasteful. This is a rather old building I'm hiding behind, all things considered. The region La Bobo Cree is mostly stainless steel nowadays, with sleek white sky-scraping towers and homes powered by solar panels. The only time you need to be next to a thing so unpleasant, rotten, and dusty is when you're in the dark shadows, hiding. Or in my case, waiting for the moment where I finally decide to step into the black market for the first time. Only my minuscule amount of confidence accompanying me. Just move one foot after another, it's not that hard. Truthfully just being on the back road of an ancient city gives me the feeling of uncertainty and sends goosebumps throughout my body. An empty sand path blowing over, leading to nothing but trouble in my perspective. Even though I'm only 5 miles away from the main street. It's so different from modern La Bobo Cree. This is old and impoverished living. If this was on the grid still, it would turn into a red light district. You know, just the icing on the cake of what is already despicable. Deep breaths Audrey. You can get through this I tell myself.

I pray to the gods of Alfralon "Juku noe pleu." God give me strength and courage. Don't look down on me for stepping into the unknown territory. I must do this for everyone's sake, mostly my own but still. I watch the creatures fly, walk, and slither around the market as if this is completely normal. Almost as if it was some small open produce market for the public, and not some run down shabby criminal area on a back street. Which by the way, you could be sentenced to death if you're caught shopping in. Even though this small corner of La Bobo Cree technically shouldn't exist.

I pull my light weight tanzanite colored coat closer to me for comfort. Why did I think I could do this again? Oh right, because if I ever wanted to actually break into the lower chambers of the planet's capital Bagoa, and save the people of Xyron. This is the where I should start. I must see if the stories are true. If I don't find out. Nothing will change

among the 6 regions. Well eventually everyone will die…
every human, every Opius, every creature, dropping one by
one. The stacks of corpses building daily. All forms of life
eventually vanishing before my eyes. Something that
couldn't be allowed to happen in my lifetime. Peeking out
from around the corner I scope out the marketplace to see if
there is a specific stand I should head over to. I'm not able to
waste another minute. While looking over the two rows of 12
tables one seems to stick out the most. It's most likely to have
the items I need.

The table was made of a burnt redwood and looked unstable
from the way it was slightly swaying left to right. It's
merchant facing away from the table, tall in a dark-colored
velvet cloak hiding them self almost completely. The table
decorated with artifacts and idols of the 6 regions and the
unknown. Skulls and creatures staring at you making you
want to turn away because you can almost hear the screams
still lingering. Live mice wandering on its table top. Eye
catching would be an understatement. Somehow it was only

the 2nd creepiest table in the entire black market. However,
the most likely to have a venomous specimen.

Something heavily tugs on my cloak behind me. My
heart jumps a bit when I turn around to see what is pulling
at my cloak. A NiCamon is looking up at me with its white
blue-tinted eyes holding a jar filled with eyeballs. They shift

around in the container, the blue, green, and gray eyes looking at me as I just wonder. Where did he get all these eyes? The Trogonese war in Belfrite was about 400 years ago and yet there were so many well-preserved eyes in this single jar from the fallen victims. I bent down staring in the fascination of this once in a lifetime opportunity. I tapped the jar lightly. He pulls away wrapping his pale white arms around the clear jar and bares his little razor sharp teeth. "Bhu gunfa lact beh te lu." he says in a stern voice in NiCamoNay giving me the evil eye.

"I'm sorry I didn't mean to upset you," I say genuinely.

His origins are from the south from what I can tell. Only the Alfralon gods know why they are so touchy and easily upset. Though to be fair standing around on the outskirts of a black market, for all he knows I might be trying to steal it. These eyes are quite the commodity. They'd be lovely to own and dangerous to have. After all, in the Belanox religion, these eyes are deemed sacred. The eyes of the native people and comrades in the Trogonese war had these eyes. When the war ended the people almost extinct and the eye colors rare.

"Na bri. Con ku."

I apologize once again.

He steps back and looks me up and down.

4

Great, I've gone and caused trouble. This is also taking up too much of my time I have scorpions I need to buy. Deadly scorpions. If this continues to go on we'll be here for a while and that will be time wasted and not an ounce of progress made. I smile at the NiCamon.

"Twu, con ku. Ku qu ma?"

"Bi bunga wa!" he says happily as he lowers his guard "Bi bunga wa, Alfies."

I dig in my brown leather pouch and pull out 35 Alfies. Which apparently is all I have left. God darn him. But truth be told, had I just walked in the market and bought what I needed and left. We wouldn't have crossed paths. So it's my own fault. Now I've caused him trouble and inconvenienced myself. I pay the NiCamon. He hands me the jar of sacred eyeballs. He recounts the money and reminds me that there are no returns. I tell him that I'm aware of the terms of purchase. He begins jumping for joy and doing a happy dance. I smile but think to myself well at least one of us is happy. As he should be, 35 Alfies is a lot in Xyron's economy today. He spits at my feet and leaves with pleasure. Then I truly begin to smile because he has done the NiCamon gesture of "pleasure of doing business with you. I will say good things about you to many people."

Alright now that the transactions over with back to the original goal. Buying my deadly scorpions. I stand up straight and put my new rare assets in my bag and straighten myself out. Starting by closing the bag, making sure my cloak covers me as much as possible, pull my white hair back, and putting on the hood of the cloak. Alright, it's now or never. I walk into the market.

When arriving at the dreadful stand with the mysterious merchant I observe the contents of the table more clearly as if for the first time. The tribal whistle beads from Crowel, a goat's head from Zovoe, singing bowls from Bolyen. This merchant has been around the world and must have gone to hell and back to get these items. The years it took to acquire such things is beyond belief. Focus Audrey, focus. We are looking for deadly scorpions I tell myself repeatedly. My hands wander over every item barely touching them and it catches my eyes. A closed black box with illegible green hieroglyphics or just extremely strange scriptures. I reach out for the box ready to buy it on the spot. At that very moment, a heavy-handed fuzzy paw comes down and grabs my wrist. It's 6-inch onyx pointed nails reaching almost halfway up my arm. Making me freeze in my tracks. Hesitantly I tilt my head upward to look up at the merchant. Long fur like a terrier dog but you can still see the wrinkles through a few of the lighter areas of fur. I've never seen this type of creature before in La Bobo Cree which is another terrifying thought.

"Go gyn nala ju. Paq de veh yin? Sed twa mah?" she says to me.

"Sed twa?"

"These are very rare and poisonous serpents, not a toy. These are for people who wish others harm. You must be very careful if you are to buy them. As well as extremely careful. NOT for children."

"I'm 23," I state to her clearly giving her a firm look "I can handle it."

"So be it," she says "they cost 80 Alfies."

Venomous snakes were not a part of my plan to restoring Xyron to peace. But it will do. Not to mention I just gave away all my money on my last unplanned transaction. Well, I guess there's only one thing I can do. I pull my hands off the table silently scraping a few beads for sale on the table into my hand and reaching for my bag as if to pull out money. I whisper to myself *la craz vu*. A minor illusion trick, my grandfather Lycrane taught me as a child. Before he was deemed dead that is by Neelia, one of the council members who helps run Xyron. I'd like to say I've perfected it since then but it only last five minutes. I quickly hand the money to the merchant who in return gives me my weapons for later. A deadly sting of poison.

I turn away quickly and walk through the crowd. While I was making the purchase it must have turned into rush hour in here. I can hardly see which way I'm headed and who I'm passing. I run into something hard and tall. I look up and my hood falls from my head. Oh no a Poldano. A species half polar bear half human. I see all her distinct features no mistaking it. She has long wavy white hair, smooth black slick skin, and extremely dark navy blue eyes. She grabs the wrist of my right arm and holds it above me and then snatches the box from my grasp.

"You have stolen from me! This is mine."
I look around frantically in every direction hopelessly. When I hear a table flip over. Soon I realize it's the merchant I bought the box from. She destroyed her own table. She hightails it out of here before she can get dragged into this. Lucky son of a bitch. Getting off scotch free for selling me the stolen goods. Just my luck. This can't be happening. Please don't say it. Please just let me go.

"I, Goona Tocra, Declare by the law of Xyron that this Opius is my new slave. Does anyone object?" she announces. She looks down at me and smiles. She's proud of herself I'm sure. Though I am dangling from her grasp and dying of public humiliation and am now in debt to her for my entire lifetime. She as a Poldano in the Belanox religion has just moved up in ranking. The Belanox religion is known for slavery and having 600 is a goddess. So I'm sure she feels quite lucky.

She whispers through a smile "No owner I see."
Taking out her whip from her belt loop she doesn't hit me
with it but ties it around my wrist. Tightly at that for
someone who did it with only one hand. She then finally lets
me go letting me drop to the ground on my knees in front of
everyone who is watching. Dragging me through the sand
my knees burn and tears begin to form in my eyes. Rocks
and bits of sand engrave themselves in my knee. And after a
bit start tearing skin, in turn, causing me to bleed and let out
whimpers in pain. I scramble to get on my feet never being
able to get it quite right. Every time I get close to holding
myself up with dignity she pulls tighter on the whip. I end
up a stumbling mess all over again. Do the Alfralon gods
have any mercy?

She drags me across town through our sandy streets. People
don't look around in wonder or bother to question. But in
the back of their heads, they feel sorry for me. It's a
nightmare being enslaved to a Poldano. Some find it so bad
that the suicide rate and physician-assisted suicide rating
has skyrocketed in the last year. Creatures are dropping left
and right and it's not just because of the economy. The
townspeople of La Bobo Cree not only feel sorry for me but
wonder if they'll ever see me again. It's amazing how one of
the things I'm fighting against, is a trap I've got myself
tangled up in. Now I'm going to experience the Councils

mistake first hand.

My legs are numb I can hardly stand. My feet bruised and red. The heat cooking my skin faster than eggs on a sidewalk. Beads of sweat dripping from my forehead. We must have walked at least 10 miles. Mouth dry and bitter with a slight taste of sand. Not offered the tiniest bit of water. Does she treat all of her slaves like this? Doesn't she at least want her slaves to survive?

"We are almost there, don't worry." says Tocra. Minutes later we stop in the middle of the sandy desert. She looks around. No, she couldn't be. Is she lost? She better not be lost. Has she just been walking aimlessly this entire time? Was she just saying that? I mean we are almost where? It's literally the middle of nowhere. There isn't a building in sight! What could she possibly be looking for? Calm down Audrey, I'm sure she knows where she's going. She wouldn't walk all this way for nothing. You're getting yourself worked up over nothing. Don't give up now.

"It's this way." she says through her thick Poldano accent; though it sounds like she's been around plenty of Russian humans.

Ms. Tocra, my owner, turns and approaches me. She starts unwrapping her tight whip from my arms. It feels pleasant because it's not cutting off my blood circulation any longer. It's no longer digging into my skin like a cat with sharp claws. She looks down at me with a look of confusion.

"Come on." she says blankly.

I follow her until she randomly stops. She stares at the ground below her. I'm so confused and I can't imagine what's running through her mind. Are we just gonna sleep here for tonight on the hot sand? So many unanswered questions. I'd ask her but Poldano's are creatures who don't like being questioned and demand respect. More importantly, I don't want to be hit with her whip.

She starts to slide around the hot sand with her foot. Revealing a wooden door with a black handle on the right side. She bends down and grabs the handle and opens the door. She reaches into her pocket and throws a ratty old purple rag at me. I catch it just barely before it hits the floor. It's my turn to give her a look of confusion.

"It's a blindfold. Wrap it around your head."

I follow her instructions. Wrapping the rag around my face I notice this powerful smell of lavender. Why does it need to smell like lavender? I choose not to make a comment and just go with it. No need to clutter my brain with trivial details. Moving forward.

"Okay, I'm finished. Now what?"

She grabs my arms once again and we descend down a staircase. She quickly latches the door shut at the last minute. I may not know where I am, but I feel goosebumps begin to rise throughout my body. It's freezing down here. Where are we? It's like the inside of a freezer. What is the A/C on?

"Don't talk. Don't make a sound."

We begin walking across a flat landscape. But we end up making a lot of turns. I'm more than happy I didn't run into anything or stub my toe.

"OK, we go upstairs now. Up."

When we reach the top of the stairs we come to a sudden stop. From what my ears can tell she lifts a wooden bar and opens a door. She leads me into the unknown room. She is close behind me. The door creaks and shuts with a thud of its own.

"You can take your blindfold off now."

I slowly remove the blindfold revealing a bedroom. A small cozy and cramped bedroom. It has about 6 bunk beds. Only 2 are empty, I assume that I'm here to fill one and she has the other.

"You sleep over there now. We start work at 9 tomorrow morning."

Chapter 2

Ms. Tocra has us all walking in line chained. My skin is
burning, my cloak was stolen, and my pride was gone. How
did I stray so far from my goal? All my plans have
completely veered left. There's a heat wave, yet somehow,
out of all of us, I'm the only one sweating. No one has said a
word this entire time. Not the other slaves, Ms. Tocra, nor
the leech carrying the rusty shovels. This woman wants to
kill us, all of us. I can feel myself slowly going mad. We stop
abruptly and the leech unlocks us one by one and hands us
our shovels.

"Alright! Get started, dig your holes," she screams like
a drill sergeant.
Everyone scatters and picks a random spot and begins
shoveling. Looking at the sand I start to outline a perfect
circle, so I can see where to start my hole and make sure to
not cover it with sand. I begin digging with all my might.

Stabbing the ground repeatedly. My hands wrapped around the shaft my knuckles turn white. My fingertips turning red ignoring the pain. My feet shifting with every other shovel. Hot sand seeping between my bare toes.

Screaming in my head "No! Why is this happening?" *stab*. "This isn't fair." *stab*. "It wasn't supposed to end like this." *stab*. The wooden shaft of the shovel starts to splinter off, it's not long before I stab myself.1, 2, 3 splinters in my hand from stabbing the ground. What does it matter anyway if I'm not out achieving my goal? There's no pain greater than that. People are suffering and dropping like flies as I'm forced to stand here in the hot ass sun digging pointless holes.

A gooey substance begins to creep down my hand and onto the shaft. When I look at it more closely, I come to find it's my blood and sweat staining the dark brown wood slowly.

I stab the shovel so it stands straight up in the ground. I probably shouldn't be stopping unless I want a lash. But I can't help but think how I'm here. I'm not in the bottom chambers of the planet's capital. Not saving the families of this horror. This never-ending nightmare. I don't completely blame anyone for the current situation. It's just that, Xyron and Neelia, the heads of our council haven't made a single good decision since they've been there. Aside from the physician-assisted suicide by local creatures, using moxus for the injection. They've cut down 40% of their donations to help small businesses for no reason. No one knows where the money went or why it disappeared. One day we woke up and Neelia made an announcement that they needed to reduce funding for council purposes. Or should I say reasons that will remain confidential to the public but has been agreed upon by the council it's for the peoples best interest.

However, the economy had been doing better than ever. Business was booming. Poverty was at an all time low. So why pull the funds? Was there a war coming? Were the lands finally going to fight again, due to sacred unresolved problems? So many questions and not a single one answered.

I just want to make it to the tower. I won't ever get it standing around here. I'll demand to see the council when I get there. Even if the folktale doesn't work I want answers. Maybe the people of Xyron haven't thought about it. Or they have but don't have an alternative solution so no one said anything. But something will be done. The people have a right to know the truth, right? Shaking my head to rid of the negative but true thoughts.

I begin to dig again. Thankfully no one noticed I stopped in the first place. No lashes for me. That's one thing to smile about. Maybe the gods are looking after me. Now that's a comforting thought. All of a sudden my insides feel warm and cozy. The sun doesn't bother me as much as it use to.

"*Shi mandu dre, kay iso bai, ni nah, bobo lan~*" a little human girl sings.

When I look at her I see a small fragile girl. Bright blue eyes filled with hope and joy despite her current circumstances. Her platinum blonde hair with a french braid to the side in the front. A face lightly covered with speckles of sand from working. Her lips a light sugary pink but drying out with every passing second. Her clothes mostly tattered and wrinkled. Yet she was here digging holes with a smile. Singing one of the most famous hymns; Bobo Lani, from the Alfralon Religion which speaks of life happily transforming. How interesting. I look at her.

"Hello, My names Audrey. What's your name?" I ask.

"Trixie." she answered while digging.

"That's a pretty name." I say bending down to get on her level "How old would you be?"

"I'm only 10." stated Trixie.

She is only a child. How could anyone take advantage of a 10-year-old girl and work her to the bone in these conditions? The world is twisted and cruel, we know. We just don't realize how much so until it slaps us in the face I guess. Did she truthfully deserve to be here? How does she make it through this? Is she hurting on the inside? Is that why she was singing a song about peace returning to the motherland. As I contemplate Trixie says something.

"Audrey," she says "you better get back to diggin."
"Is that so?"

"Yeah, don't let Ms. Tocra catch you taking a break. She'll give you a good lashing."
"I see," I tell her as I stand up straight.

"Not to mention you're not digging your holes properly either. You're suppose to dig them deep, not long. If she uses the holes you dig, her treasures would be stolen." she whispers the last part.

My curiosity reaching its peak, I began to think. How does a 10-year-old know so much about digging holes? The way the slave owner prefers them. She seems to know a lot for her age.

I notice that the hole she's been digging is about 1 foot wide and 3 feet deep. Quite efficient and quick for a child. I'm afraid to ask, but I must know. I need to know for certain.

"Trixie," I began "How long have you been out here? How long have you been working for Ms. Tocra ?"

She looks at me and then proceeds to raise an eyebrow. She begins counting on her fingers. She doesn't say any actual numbers though.

"Well...I started working here when I was 5. I'm 10 now. So how long has it been?"

She can't count, is the first thing that comes to mind. The second is she's been working since the age of 5. This is more or less all she knows. Five years have passed and she doesn't even know it. I don't want to explain to her how long that is. But I'm sure she realizes it's been a very long time. "Anyway, I ended up here because my mommy lost me. She was gambling again and lost me in a bet. Mommy didn't have any money. So here I am. Digging holes and being raised by Ms. Tocra. She's a good person deep down. Ms. Tocra is like my second mom."

I feel sorry for her. I try to give her a lighthearted smile. But my eyes are beginning to water on me. My heart is clutching and causing a pain. Don't be so emotional I tell myself. She's a tough little girl. So many reasons in Xyron's society is messed up. More reasons to make it to the castle. This girl deserves to be free. Not saying she needs to go back to her no good mother but she doesn't necessarily deserve to be enslaved either.

Trixie states "Lady, you ask a lot of questions. You better get to work. I'm not trying to be mean or scare you. But if she catches us she's gonna give us a lashing. And I already have two."

She pulls up the left sleeve of her tattered brown shirt

that's barely staying together. She reveals a glowing purple mark. Two S-shaped lashes that make an interesting § mark. I look towards Ms. Tocra and her whip. It's different compared to the one from the other day. It has a skull based handle, and it's glowing from dark magic. She beats her slaves with enchanted whips? Oh Trixie, there's nothing nice about that. You need another mother figure. Cause what you've been exposed to just isn't right.

Trixie and I start digging in sync. *Shove, toss, shove, toss*. It seems as if it was a million shove and tosses later that a whistle was sounded and Trixie explained to me that meant the work day was over. What a helpful little girl she is. All of the slaves including myself form a single file line. Wait ! Did I just admit to being a slave? Clank. The handcuffs shut around my wrist, bringing me back to reality. Ms. Tocra tells us that we're headed back. This time we aren't blindfolded. Which for some reason is making my skin crawl. I thought I wanted to know where we came and went. Now that it's happening I'm not so sure.

 We end up back at the wooden door I had seen before, last night. Wooden, shitty, and with a black handle. I'm not sure I completely understand what's going on. But she's the one in charge. Better not to question things I'm sure. Even when it seems that it makes absolutely no sense.

"Welcome home. Today you will be doing part 2 of your

shift."

How can you have part 2 of a shift? Isn't a shift a shift? That also makes no sense. She didn't even say what we were doing. She does realize I'm new here right?

The leech unlocks the handcuffs one by one taking his sweet time. With every undoing, a creature descends the stairs trying to hide some type of dread. It's finally my turn to go. Heading over to the unknown, cold air hits my skin. It's negative 30 degrees down there. Noticing the walls were made of ice. An underground cave of solid ice. I slowly walk down the hall. Wouldn't want to slip and hurt myself.

Ms. Tocra says from behind me "Welcome to Diamonds Vibe Inn ice pub. You will be waitress here. You shall wear this as your uniform."

She throws an outfit over my shoulder. It consists of a red tight short fitted kimono. With the top being a laced hex star. But the flowy sleeves traditional. What is this place? "You will be serving drinks to the most wanted smugglers on the planet. So try to do your best. Good luck. You will have to change in the bathroom which is around the corner from the bar. So hurry and get to work. You must earn your keep here."

Doing everything she tells me in the order she tells me gets me on the floor quicker than I expected. This outfit keeps me surprisingly warm for it's lacking in fabric. When I

20

get to the bar a bartender is already handing me a platter of drinks. I'm just happy he didn't scratch me with his scaly arms in the process.

"Two Bonnie Bon Bon's and a Bloody Sunday." he screams yelling out to the crowd not caring if my ear drum shatters.

"Over here. That's us." a speckled beard toad calls. "I'm coming," I say nervously while walking, my foot catches on something.

Bam ! ! ! The platter of drinks crash to the ground. I hit the floor almost bashing my face in. When looking up I see nothing but centipedes floating in its pink lemonade mixing with the radioactive worms from the wasted Bonnie bon bon drinks.

The smugglers, I mean customers don't give me a second look. Which is a good thing I suppose. Less embarrassing on my end. Scrambling to get to my feet a Cralu comes by. Eating all the glass and worms cleaning up my mess. Thank the Alfralon gods for the little elephant-cockroach breed.

Running back over to the bar the waiter already has a new platter for me to deliver. Pacing myself this time going slower than before someone shouts "Hey new girl!" I spin around and accidentally hit a customer with a platter. He's upset and has the drinks spilled all over his clothes. Ms. Tocra pulls me away quickly before he can say a word. Or in this type of environment, lay a hand on me.

"Okay, that's enough out of you. You obviously can't deliver or serve a simple drink. So now you *dance*." she says to me in a strict but nervous tone.

I must have screwed up if her voice is wavering. Sounds like I have something to make up for. Or we are both dead. Just get it together already would you.

How? There's a tower waiting for me to invade it. A planet secretly wanting to be saved. And yet here everyone is enjoying themselves in an enchanted underground pub. As if nothing is going on and people of their race aren't dropping by the second.

Time is passing and Ms. Tocra is getting a look on her face. One not quite describable. The imaginary clock begins to tick in my head. *Tick, tick, tick.* You're supposed to be making a change. But what is one to do? Run and risk being lashed or worst beheaded on the spot. *Tick, tick, tick.* To make matters even more unpleasant. I've made a friend. Trixie. So young. What will she think if she sees me do this sinful thing? *Tick, tick, tick.* Is there a way to get out of this situation? Can I ask Ms. Tocra for another job? How could I manage to do something like that? *Tick, tick, tick, tock.* She reaches for the skull handle of her whip.

Chapter 3

Before she has a firm grip on the handle I head for the women's bathroom once again to change. I make sure to get it done in a timely manner. Even though I'm nervous and I'm shaking with fear. I can only think of how long it has been since this last occurred. There wasn't a single day that I woke up and thought I would have to relive this moment. All the torture. The screaming.

My stomach turns abruptly. Memories flooding my brain. Bile threatens to come up but I manage to keep it down. You're almost at the stage. Keep walking and you'll be in the clear.

I climb onto the platform with ease. Soon as I stand center stage I freeze. All eyes locked on me. My feet are now cinder blocks. Body slightly moistening. My eyes batting like crazy.

Scanning the room I see the other dancers in cages doing moves that require a lot of flexibility. A starting point.

The crowd silent. Waiting for me to stop looking like a deer in head lights.

"COME ON! We ain't got all day." yells a smuggler in the crowd with octopus legs.

Looking in the direction of the voice I find myself making the hugest mistake. My eyes. They land on Trixie's. She's looking at me. I don't want to disappoint her. I don't want her to see this. I won't do this in front of her. That's when Trixie's eyes change. The emotion changing. Changing to an anxiousness. Almost as if she's telling me to hurry up. It's OK if she sees me like this. Oh, Trixie. I'm sorry.

Shying away from the crowd and Trixie, I turn my head. Closing my eyes I take a deep breath. The live band starts to play some seductive jazz music. That's when it all came back. Completely remembering everything I once was forced to do. To please them. Opening my eyes, I let my muscle memory take over.

Slowly I peer over my shoulder and give the smuggler that called out at me earlier a cutesy little wink. That alone seems to have caught his attention. Running my fingers upwards through my smooth silky white hair. They're all frozen in awe. Not long after I find myself move, groove, and grinding to the beat of the music. Of course, I throw a high kick in every now and then.

The crowd loves me. The whistling. The clapping of tentacles. The flapping of wings. Let's not forget the stomping of hooves. Which is good for them. They're enjoying themselves. Which means they're turned on and I won't get any lashings. But I drown in my own self-hatred. Focus on the music. Keep your attention on the music. You're doing great. Positive thinking will keep you from crying, later on, I think to myself. Attempting to change my mindset.

"Oh, the things I would do to her." I overhear someone tell their friend in the crowd.
Confirmation that all eyes are on me. I'm proud and disappointed. Happy and sad. My body is just a whirlpool of emotions. But it'll be ok in the end. If it ever ends.

Just then the smuggler waves me over. This guy wants a private show. Which means I better get over there fast. When the beat drops I switch over to belly dancing. Slowly approaching him as I dance. Not only to keep him under my spell. But to hide.
Hiding all of my nerves. From the shaking in my feet. Trembling of the toes. Palms twitching. None of that matters because he's focused on my perfect execution of the famous belly roll. Since it is appealing to the eye his focus and everyone else is purely on my stomach. No one notices.

I can't shake away the memories but I was forever

trying back then.

$$\dagger \qquad \dagger \qquad \dagger$$

It's late at night and I'm hiding in my room under my sparkly pink covers. Hoping to fall asleep before they come for me. I just want to go to sleep like a regular nine-year-old girl. One who goes to school, gets good grades, prays to the Alfralon gods at night, and then goes to sleep. Then do it all again the next day like a broken record.

But that never seems to happen for me. Especially if it's poker night at our house. Those are the nights that things are the worst for me. It's when the nightmares begin.

Poker nights usually involve my grandpa Lycrane's friends coming over. Their names are Monk and Sammy. They come and do unspeakable things to me. When grandpa's awake it's regular poker. But when he's asleep after drinking a lot of beers and alcohol. Monk and Sammy make me entertain them for the night. They claim they have nothing to do now that he's sleeping. But they do, they can go home to their wives and kids. But they don't. They stay and pick on me. They force me to play strip poker. I don't like it but I'm too small and too young. It's not like I can beat them up. I've tried yelling but no one comes to my rescue. If grandpa's other friends are here they're passed out drunk as well. That or they choose to ignore my screams and just go home altogether. So I always get stuck with them.

I clench my Barbie covers tighter around me making sure it covers my entire body. Building a cocoon of safety. My shield from the darkness but not necessarily the monsters.

A shadowy figure burst through the door making a loud bang. I can't make out whether it's Monk or Sammy. But what's the difference their both the same kind of monster. No not tonight I begin to think to myself. Didn't I suffer enough yesterday. I bought all the drinks on time. I even did the dance they forced me to learn. I did what they said. But they still want more from me, my fragile body is still sore from last nights events.

The shadowy figure staggers towards me knocking stuff off the dresser in the process. I squeeze my eyes shut. If I close my eyes he'll disappear. I know it's not true but I still don't want to see exactly who it is. I don't need to have my eyes open for any of this. But when I hear a second person coming I reluctantly open my eyes.

Just as this happens I realize it's Monk at the foot of my bed. He managed to stand up straight. If Monk is at the foot of the bed that means it's Sammy standing guard by my door. When I make this connection Monk rips the sheets off of me and throws it in the direction of the door in one fluid motion. Sammy kicks the sheet until it's out of the room, then proceeds to lock the door. It traps me in my room with a loud click. Nowhere to run and nowhere to hide. Just me in my room with my grandpa's friends. This isn't right I tell myself. I shouldn't have to go through this.

"It's late, and your grandpa is finally asleep. So it's time for us to play our favorite game." Monk states with a smirk on his face.

"Can we not play the game?" I say warily "I'm really tired."

"Don't pretend you don't like it." he screams "You know I hate *when you say that."*

Monk slaps me heavy-handed across the face and my head hits the headboard. I raise my hand to my mouth. My cheek is swelling and my lip is bleeding. Bruising forming on my forehead. Monk doesn't care. He loves the torture. He loves to see me in pain. He slams his calloused hands on to my ankles and digs his dirty yellow nails into them. Then drags me closer to the foot of the bed towards him. I scream in pain not that it helps my situation.

"Oh please scream. I love it when you scream. The more you scream. The more you'll make it worth my while."

After I'm out of breath and tears are forming in my eyes. I start clawing at his hands locked into my ankles. Continuously trying to peel them back and pry them off. Ultimately it's useless. He's too strong and my hands are so small and weak. I'm only nine after all. I cry frantically when I realize there is no escaping his grasp. I'm just not strong enough.

Sammy decides to walk towards the head of the bed. He grabs my hands so I can't claw at Monk's hands anymore. There is nothing I can do. I can't fight them. It's all over. I surrender, I give up.

When Sammy has a firm and solid grip on both my wrist he looks at Monk. Monk then gives me a wicked smile. He stands at the foot of the bed making sure I can see him. Forcing me to watch him undress himself. First, he unbuttons his red plaid shirt and lets it float to the floor. Next, he pulls his white undershirt off and over his head letting it plop where ever it pleases. Then he unbuckles his black leather belt and slides it out of the notches of his jeans. He lets his jeans, belt, and boxers drop all with a big thud. He does all this while never breaking eye contact with me.

When he's finished undressing himself. It's my turn. He removes my sneakers one by one. Slides off my fluffy socks with bells on them. Wiggles me out of my tight jeans. Then when I'm down to practically nothing. He tears off my panties and throws them aside like trash.

I'm overwhelmed and nothing can stop me from feeling this way. No matter how many times I go through this. My heart is racing and my legs are trembling as I ball my hands up into a fist. Just make it stop. Make it all end. Grandpa wake up I plead. If you were awake you would make it stop. You would never let this happen again. Not to your favorite little princess. I know you wouldn't. Cause you're a hero. Heroes take out the bad guys.

They're your friends. I get that, I do. But bad guys are bad guys. So wake up and save me already. Beat up the bad guys like the hero you are.

Monk climbs on top of the bed acting like the predator he is. As I lay here as his helpless prey. He hovers above me, motionless. Just staring at me with his black orbs he calls eyes. My body is just frozen in fear that all movement has stopped. The world and time itself have stopped. My voice mute. Everything is quite. All I can feel is Monk above me. All I can smell is the beer and vodka that he reeks of. The world starts up again. When everything is back in motion. He positions himself to be more comfortable on top of me. Then starts to pleasure himself by rubbing his sex up and down against mine.

"Stop it," I cry "You're disgusting. You're a disgusting sinner."

"I'm fine with that. God will forgive me for my sins," he says sure of himself.

"I can't wait for him to send you straight to hell. Cause that's the only place you're going" I state.

"I'm fine with that too." he responds.

I moisten my mouth and spit on him. Yeah, I know better. Grandpa told me to never do that. But Monk deserves to be disrespected. The man is a pig. He's taking advantage of a helpless 9-year-old. How sick and twisted do you have to be? Not to mention he's cocky about it as well.

Crashing his rough un-hydrated lips against mine I make a disgusted sound. He forces his tongue into my mouth. Running his hands through my long white hair. More of his body weight on me now. My punishment for disrespecting him. Being forced to taste the beer, alcohol, and fresh smoked cigars.

Not only that but he takes his left hand and runs it slowly down my face. Touching my cheek, my neck, all the way down my side and stopping at my waist. He slips his large cold hands under my yellow and blue striped shirt and travels up till he reaches my undeveloped breast.

I try to toss and turn. Trying to squirm out of his grasp. This isn't fair. I didn't ask for this. I didn't want this for myself. Do the Alfralon gods have no mercy? It doesn't work. Another attempted fail on my part.

"This isn't right," I state.

"What isn't right. Is that you haven't made me feel alright yet," he replies.

"Not to mention I still haven't had my turn to be satisfied for the night," Sammy says making his presence known.

Monk picks up where he left off. Groping my undeveloped chest.

Watching and enjoying my facial expressions of horror. How does he sleep with himself at night? Honestly, I think he'd give the devil a run for his money. I think the Alfralon gods would agree that there's nothing more wicked that walks the lands. Then Monk himself.

Time passes. I don't know how much. Or how little. I just know that it is. There's nothing I can say or do. I'm just here. I'm just a nine-year-old girl being used for someone else's pleasure. To be used at their disposal. I'm just here. They took turns the rest of the night. All I could think is that I learned one thing. In the end...after it all ended. I learned that at the very least. Monsters don't live under the bed.

✝   ✝   ✝

The smuggler's bat wing wraps around me out of nowhere. His touch bringing me back to reality and far away from that dreadful night. Even though it still feels all the same. He didn't need to hold me so close. But I can't complain. So I just go with it.

He announces to everyone in the pub "Sorry guys, the show is over. For the rest of the night, she's my girl. We'll be in a private room. So if you need me...well, don't need me." Is he suppose to be important or something? I don't recognize him. He must want to look good in front of his friends. But if it's a private room he wants. A private room he will get. Before I even get the chance he started "lightly" guiding me toward the private rooms himself. So much for that.

When we arrive at the private room. He picks the one at the end of the hall on the left. Which for some reason seems to be warmer if you ask me. I wonder if he knows that. Pushing the ice sleet door open I reveal a room with an ice dancing pole on the right. A soft and comfy looking 3 seater couch on the left. Little white lights lining the ceiling. It is beautiful and bare.

Walking over to the pole the smuggler takes his seat. He relieves a deep sigh. This guy I just can't tell. Is he working hard or hardly working? I mean we are in a back room. No need to act tough now. Unless...it isn't an act. He introduces his self "My name is Vevro."

As he talks I dance on the pole. Swaying around it. More tricks I performed as a child. Now I'm using more of my upper body strength than my legs. Which opens me up to more of a variety. With the variety of tricks, I can throw together. I'm sure I can keep myself entertained and distracted as well. But I make sure to keep an open ear just in case he makes a request. Or tries anything suspicious and or life threatening.

"I am a top drug dealer. Well we're in a private room so no

need to be humble about it, right? I *am* Belfrite's top drug dealer. By the way, don't worry I know the rules. No touching, So I talk. I hear you very hard-working girl." he says.

When and where did he hear that crap? Was he paying attention when I dropped all those drinks. Hard-working people don't put effort into dropping stuff. They put effort into balancing it. Not to mention there's a child out on the floor who digs holes better than I do. He is obviously talking about some other girl. Cause hard-working is something I don't see myself as. Especially in his line of work.

"Now before you say anything. Just listen. I want to do business with you. You seem like quick learner from what I have witnessed tonight. I see much potential in you. Even though you bit clumsy. But it's ok Vevro forgives you."

Is he serious? He wants to do business with me. Why would I want to work for him? A drug dealer. The top smuggler. Vevro is very strange if he wants me around.

"Plus I no make you do deliveries. You be my own private very special dancer. No slave work for you. I promise. You can trust me. Don't worry about a thing. If you no like it then you don't have to work for me. You can continue doing your work for Ms. Tocra. But I will be back in a week. Then you will give me another private show. And tell me the answer to my offer. OK? You know I really like you. You don't talk much and don't ask any questions. You good. Very good."

‡   ‡   ‡

Chapter 4

It's been four days and I still haven't come to a conclusion about Vevro's offer. I mean what am I suppose to make of all this? It's no one's dream to be a private dancer for a smuggler. But no one wants to be a slave in a chain gang either. Neither of those things is pleasant. They both don't pay well either. Actually, they don't pay at all. If I am with Vevro I wonder if I'd get more breaks. I wouldn't be shoveling aimlessly. Would I be sleeping in a monitored room somewhere when I wasn't dancing? Who is to say?

Is there really any sense in changing owners, to begin with. A slave is a slave, right? I still have no freedoms or rights. Even though Vevro did make my work with him seem more laid back. He may be a Bapus. But he seemed like a good guy. You know outside of his smuggling business. But hey I guess you have to be charismatic to be where he is right? I bet he never ended up in slavery. He never got

35

sidetracked from his goal. Make money and do what he
wants.

"Audrey, are you okay?" Trixie asks "Your shoveling like you
have somewhere better to be?"

"Maybe I do have places to be. " I insinuate.

"Where could you possibly be going?"

"To the capital," I state.

"You mean Bagoa. Bagoa, Zovoe," she says giving me an
odd look.

"Yes, Bagoa." I smile.

"What are you going to do when you get there?" she
questions me.

"I'm gonna get there. Enter the layer. And take down
the bad guys."

She laughs at me in response. Does she think I'm some type
of looney? Does she think the heat is finally starting to get to
me? Though to be honest I did make it sounds like a fairy
tale for her. Practically pretending that she hasn't been
exposed to the things she has.

"That sounds far-fetched don't you think? Sounds like
the famous folktale too. But most importantly, you don't talk
like an adult at all. You sound like a twelve-year-old. If it
was possible. I would want to go too. It sounds like a fun
adventure. Plus I've never been outside of La Bobo Cree. I've
only heard of what Bagoa is like. I want to see it in person

though."

"Really? Well, I'm sure you'll get there someday."

"I don't know. In a strange way, I'd think i'd miss Ms. Tocra. So I kinda feel conflicted because I know she'll probably never go north. I mean I've been with her forever. We've only been here and the border of Eil Poldane. She only goes between the two. She never even mentions the other regions."

"Is that so?"

"Yeah."

"I don't know if you realize this but you're very observant. Especially for your age."

Trixie states "Maybe it's because I'm around adults all the time."

"Your probably right," I said agreeing.

Bang, bang. I hear my shovel hitting a hard object. I feel the vibrations of the shovel. What could I be hitting with the shovel. There's nothing out here. Nothing but sand and... treasure. Trixie did say we were digging holes to bury her treasures. Is it possible that I'm hitting a treasure that was buried here? I mean when we finish we don't mark where we've already buried a treasure. Now that I think about it. We don't have a very good system. But the lady does what she wants. No point in telling her.

I start digging around the hard object that I keep hitting. I'm excited on the inside. I'm curious to know what it is. My body is running on adrenaline but I try to keep it to a minimum. Don't need anyone noticing that I'm digging faster than usual. Or that something has caught my interest. I want to keep my low profile and lash free body just the way it is. I dig and dig while occasionally hitting the object. About 15 minutes in I spot a turquoise color. I lightly brush some more sand off of it. That's odd.

Resuming to dig at a slightly yet unnoticeable pace. I realize that whatever this turquoise object is. It's definitely round. So I start digging around the edges. Keeping in mind that I need to reveal it only for my eyes to see. My eyes and no one else. Not even Trixie's. Plus, I'll need to cover it back up before we leave. Won't have enough time to cover it if I take out too much dirt. I keep that into consideration.

Eventually, I discover new details about the mysterious object. It's a turquoise orb on a stick. Is it a wand? A staff maybe? At the base of the staff, I can see a vertical metal connected to this orb. It's a silver metal with engraved symbols or a dead language. I'd like to lean in closer but that might cause the others to get suspicious. "Audrey !" Ms. Tocra yells.

"Yes," I say back in a reasonable volume.

"Why have you stopped digging? Do you have something to report," she says to me like I'm some type of corporal.

"No, Nothing to report." I state.

"Well then get back to work."

I guess I stared a second too long at the mysterious artifact because I still got in trouble. Which is just fantastic. I was being careful. I take a glimpse at Trixie. She's shaking her head as if she disapproved of something. Did she notice? Wow, I really need to work on maintaining normalcy. I need to practice keeping my facial expressions to a minimum. Maybe that will help.

Covering the orb up with particles of dust I keep in mind how I don't want to completely forget where it is. I found it and I want to keep it. Trixie and I don't say much after I had Ms. Tocra's attention drawn our way. So I spend the rest of the time listening to her hum the Bobo Lani song. The same song she sang the first day we met.

Now, what am I suppose to do? Someone, please help me. Just try not to think about it Audrey. You realize you never were good at keeping secrets, right? I remind myself. Well, this has to be a secret. Plus you're older now. So you should have no problem with, withholding information from people. You have more control of yourself now. Trying hard to reassure myself.

I finish covering it up just as Ms. Tocra calls us in. I must be getting use to being out here and doing slave work already. Who would have thought.

We get back to the Inn and head to our beds. I slide into my bunk while releasing a huge sigh. At least today we didn't work the pub. All the dancing gets tiring eventually.

As the lights go out I stare at the bottom of the bunk above me. Not only am I not tired. But everyone falls asleep in a matter of minutes. It's just me and my thoughts. Believe it or not, it ends up getting pretty quite up here even though the pub is still running downstairs directly below us. I always thought that was interesting.

I just keep thinking about how I ended up here. How my past affects me. How people say the past isn't the past if it's still affecting your present. My brain just keeps replaying memories and justifying them with a bunch of random cliches it decides to rattle off. I guess you can say I'm thinking myself to death. Not long after I drift into a deep sleep causing me to dream.

"Finally, she isn't watching and has her back turned," I whisper to myself "Looks like she'll be busy for a while."
I decide it's now or never to pull the orb from the ground. My lovely eye-catching mysterious orb. Come to me. I squat down to get closer and wrap my hands around it and start to pull it out of the ground. Pull I yell at myself, Pull. It starts sliding out of the

socket. It's longer than I expected. When it's completely out I dust off some leftover sand. Different than I expected. It is a staff like I guessed. However, it has a wooden stand. The metal I saw earlier is just a cap to connect it to the orb. Either way, it remains fascinating.

I start wielding the staff like a child playing pretend. Feeling strong and powerful. It's been a while since I've seen anyone with a staff. Taking a closer look at the wood. I finally can get a closer look at its inscriptions. Is it hieroglyphics or something else altogether? The inscriptions run throughout the entire staff head to toe. I've never seen anything like it. Must be a dead language. So I was right. There are bonuses to having the inscriptions in the staff. Other than adding mystery that is. It also seems to give it a nice fine grip.

Ms. Tocra catches me holding her treasure. My body quickly begins to moisten. My heart stops from the fear. I collapse to the ground with the lack of ability to control my legs. What's happening to me? I clutch onto my chest gasping for air. I can't breathe. The staff has hit the ground and rolled in front of me no longer in reach. Help me! I think to myself, help. My head pounding. Everything is spinning. My eyelids are growing heavy. When Ms. Tocra is only a few steps away I hit the ground with a thud.

‡   ‡   ‡

41

Chapter 5

I'm still not sure what to make of the dream I had last night. Which one is worst? That I'm afraid. Or was it the shaking and trembling I had? The fear that made me collapse to the ground. Maybe the dream was just all too real in general. In the end, a dream is a dream. This dream won't stop me or make me change my mind. I shouldn't let a silly nightmare scare me and change my mind about all this. It should be an encouragement of sorts, in a weird way. Mostly because I don't want to be that girl in the dream. The weak and fragile one. If anything is to be accomplished it's gonna take blood, sweat, and tears. A lot of hard work and it'll probably even make me uncomfortable at times. It takes courage. But it's a sacrifice I have to make. Being a better me is important. I must be a better version of myself. If not for myself, the people of Xyron. The creatures of this planet and their families. And the friends of those families.

I take my shovel and dig my hole. Trixie's just next to me humming Bobo Lani again. For a little girl, she takes her work very seriously. But somehow she always seems to make the hard work look relaxing at the same time. I'd say she's lucky but I'd be lying to myself. I look back toward the hole I'm digging to realize that I have fallen behind majorly due to daydreaming about the nightmare. I better catch up quick. Wouldn't want anyone to notice.

What's that strange sound? There's a rumbling in the distance. It sounds like a bunch of sand clots shifting. As if their vibrating against the ground. It's hard to explain.

Looking in the direction of the sound I see a lizard-drawn stagecoach wagon. It's made of mahogany wood and thin wooden wheels. The windows and doors outline with gold bead embellishments. A week worth of luggage cases tied down with rope on top of it. The lizards crawling extremely fast. They are definitely the cause of that irritating sound. But still, I wonder how the hot sand doesn't bother them. Or maybe it does and that's why their crawling so fast. Finally taking a look at the driver that's riding around in such a vehicle. I see him. It's Vevro the smuggler from the inn. What's that Bapus doing here? It's only Tuesday. Yeah, today is April 22nd. He's not supposed to see me again till the 24th. He did say that I didn't have to work with him if I

43

didn't want too. Is he here for something else? How did he even know we were out here? He's a smuggler maybe he came to buy some luxurious treasure from Ms. Tocra. I'm almost positive their good friends considering their lifestyles.

Vevro stops the stagecoach on the left side of the plot. He slithers down from his wagon and makes his way towards her. Ms. Tocra being on the right side of the plot. She's further away today because she's keeping a close eye on Dylan and Cosma. Apparently, they weren't digging holes in the right manner and she thought they needed some extra supervision.

Ms. Tocra eventually turns around and acknowledges Vevro's presence. When she sees him she opens her arms wide for a welcoming hug. I knew it they are close friends. Wait a minute, what am I doing? This is my chance to finally pull the staff out of the ground. I squat down and move some sand out of the way with my hands and start to pull. She shouldn't notice me right? She's too busy exchanging flirtatious pleasantries with Vevro.

I start to wiggle the staff out of the socket. Is it wood? Metal? Or is it something else altogether and nothing like my dream. Come out already. As I pull and tug and scan around to make sure no one sees me. My brain actually calculates the distance. Vevro and Ms. Tocra are twice as far from me. Compared to me and the billionaire stagecoach.

Should I make a break for it? Would I be able to make it? Am I willing to risk it? Is this a test of fate? This has to be a total coincidence. Things like this just don't happen. If I was to run right now I'd be able to get back to my original plans. Even if it does involve me living on the run. Assuming that I get to it before Ms. Tocra gets to me. I can make it. I'm almost positive I could make it. This could be a chance to prove myself worth. To prove to myself that I'm not the girl in that stupid dream.

The staff pops out and I analyze it for a bit. From the tip of the orb to the base of the metal staff. Being able to get a closer look at it and holding it. It's completely made up of distinct features.
The staff itself is completely engraved with a dead or unknown language. Not to mention it gives the staff an amazing grip. This must be some type of heirloom or ancient artifact. Nothing compares to this amazing work. But I'm still not a hundred percent sure what the orb is for. Why would a bow staff need an orb? It can't be for decoration. Regardless of how beautiful it is. You don't just add things if it serves no purpose.

Ms. Tocra spots me and notices that I'm not working. Even more importantly I'm holding something of value that doesn't belong to me. First she looks at me with confusion as

45

if I've lost my mind. Which slowly transforms into anger an and an unknown level of pisstivity the average brain can't comprehend. Truthfully I wouldn't be surprised if her face was secretly turning purple.

What am I doing? I dash towards Vevro's wagon and I don't look back. Not wasting another second. This is my chance. I'm going to take it. Running as fast as my bare feet and the stinging sand will allow.

The sand is sizzling the bottom of my heels. Snuggling itself between my toes. Occasionally turning into a sinkhole trying to trap me here like a vine grabbing at an ankle. But I refuse to stay here any longer. My feet can't handle the little grains of sand stabbing me in the foot but just hang in there. I think about when Vevro first pulled up, how the lizards were slithering. I just focused on that image to distract myself from the pain. If two lizards could handle it. So can I.

My heart is beating like crazy. Beads of sweat are falling off of me. Everything in this moment is just so surreal. I can't catch my breath and I'm not really pacing myself. Who cares as long as I don't collapse out of nowhere like I did in the dream. I'm going to make it. I've made it further than what I dreamt already. So I know I can do it, and anything is possible. Just watch me.

I'm sure everyone at the plot is looking at me

wondering. What the hell is she thinking? Does she have some sort of death wish? What's come over her? It's impossible, no one has ever escaped slavery from a Poldano. But maybe they're right. Maybe I'm crazy and a few screws are loose. Maybe I do have a death wish. Maybe none of the decisions I've made since I've decided to travel to Bagoa makes any sense. And it doesn't make any sense to anyone around me. But it's ok because I understand. As long as I understand the path I've decided to take that's all that matters.

My brain starts to register sound around me. I hear my feet hitting the sand in hard thumps. All the shifting sand I'm kicking up. My heart thumping in my ears. I also hear Ms. Tocra chasing me. I hear her heavy feet stomping angrily on the ground. She is more than upset. Knowing this it worries me and makes me more nervous. If she catches me I really might not make it out of here alive. There's no way I'm going to give her the opportunity though. I've worked for her longer than I would've liked. I'm definitely not going to let her take any more of my time. Or in this situation my life.

Just when I thought it couldn't get any worst than her decision to actually chase me. I hear the heavy whipping of a lash. It cracks louder than any thunder I've ever heard. Is she trying to catch me with it? Or kill me where I stand? Doesn't matter because I don't want to be the one to find out.

47

"Get back here you damn gutradon. Leave my staff!" she yells from behind.

"No, it's mine!" I shout back.

Wow. All sorts of things are revealing themselves today. Didn't know I had it in me. Mentally giving myself a satisfying pat on the back. Today I, Audrey Wakaun have made much progress. Be very proud of yourself I think.

Finally reaching the wagon I jump on and grab the reigns. Which brings me to the realization that I have no idea how to drive this thing. Nor do I have the time to figure it out when I have Ms. Tocra still running towards me. Getting a good grip on the reigns I just thrash them as hard as I can with all my strength.

The two lizards roar to life and take off way faster than the speed Vevro was going when he arrived. They run at an incredible speed faster than any vehicle I've ever been in. Which is why I almost fell over and fell off. That would have been very bad in my case.

"She actually made it." a creature from the plot yells out.

"Yes." I whisper to myself "I made it."

The lizards still slithering wildly I decide to take a guess on how to drive. I tug the reigns to the left with all my might. The lizards make my desired U-turn. I don't know which way I'm headed but who cares as long as it's away from here.

My deductive reasoning tells me that I should go the way Vevro came.Vevro's a smuggler, so he's most likely coming from a place near society. That or a place where he just finished making a deal. Either way, i'm going with my gut feeling. It gets me into trouble sometimes but it always pays off in the end.

The emotions start to take over. The grace and mercy I've received from the gods. The happiness and the feeling of freedom. The freedom I use to take for granted. Lesson learned, to say the least.

My heart returns to its normal pace. Adrenaline is falling steadily. My feet cooling down since they are no longer being abused by me and the burning sand clots.

Why do I feel so bad? That was weird. Why the sudden change of heart? The emptiness? All the joy seems to be quick to fade away. As if I was forgetting something. Oh my god Trixie. She's still there. I have to go back. If I don't the Alfralon gods will never forgive me. Hell, I'd never forgive me. I've helped myself. Now I must help her. So I make one more U- turn and head back to rescue her.

†   †   †

After I get Trixie and I feel happy this time for real.

Overwhelmingly happy I just beam rays of sunshine I'm sure. Just because she's sitting next to me while I'm driving. I know that she's safe. No more exposure to inappropriate things for her. Though I know rescuing her doesn't make up for lost time it does ensure that she won't waste anymore. I'm still not a hundred percent sure why I'm so attached. But the truth is. It doesn't matter. I helped someone in need.

"So where are we headed again?" she speaks up after a while of just riding while looking out at nothing but hills of sand.

"Bagoa." I say "The planet's capital. It's in Zovoe. Which is northeast of here. We should arrive in Bagoa in about two and a half days."

"Two and a half days!" she says shocked at my answer "When are we gonna stop? We've been driving around for hours. Literally, the sun is setting and everything." she screams.

I state "Don't worry we'll be stopping soon. The lizards need to be fed. We need to eat. So we'll stop at the North Trisector."

Trixie looks at me with a blank expression on her face. I forgot she is a bit illiterate.

I say with a smile "The North Trisector is where Belfrite, La Bobo Cree, and Eil Poldane all meet at one point. So technically you're in all three at once. So we call it the North

Trisector."

She looks at me with a sparkle in her eyes.
"That's so cool~." she says completely captivated by the idea
you can be in three places at once.

I still remember that feeling myself. When my
grandfather had told me that. It was something magical
about the idea. Even though in reality it's the idea or concept
that is beautiful. Many people come and go through the
Trisector. So there's a lot of people. But I don't know if that's
the best thing for us right now. We need to be low key.
Trixie interrupts my thoughts "Wait! Did you say La Bobo
cree, Belfrite, and Eil Poldane."

I nod my head "Yes, why?"
She responds "I remember hearing in the pub once that it
was really dangerous there. If the smugglers are saying it's
dangerous is it really safe for us to be going there."

"You're right," I state " It's very dangerous. But I'm
sure no one will bother us. Plus, I'll keep you safe. So don't
worry."
"Are you sure?" she says warily to me not completely
convinced.

"I'm absolutely positive. I won't let anything happen
to you."
"But aren't you scared? For yourself." she questions.

"No, I'm not." I lie to her.

Frankly, i'm not scared. I'm terrified. But I'm not gonna tell her that. She needs to think that she's going to be safe. The North Trisector is dangerous. It's a passing point between slave traders and smugglers. Belfrite was affected the second most when the Trogonese war hit. They have yet to recover from the poverty. Making a lot of them travel to the Trisector for the moxus injection. Or homeless beggars.

As for Eil Poldane, we just escaped from our slave owner. Hopefully, she didn't put a bounty on our heads. Hopefully, no one knows who we are. Even though no one has escaped before. There is a law saying if you do escape from them another Poldano – the one who recognizes you – is to make the decision for taking you in as their slave or putting you to death themselves.

So we can die or end up back where we started. And we are trying to run from La Bobo Cree. So there's simply no going back. We need to maintain a low profile. Which is why we are going back to where grandpa and I once stayed.

We pull up to the Trisector's gate. Yes even though it serves no real purpose and you don't need any identification or anything. Someone decided we needed a gatekeeper. The rain starts pouring on us. The thunder beginning to crackle. Lightning threatening to strike. A warm welcome as always from Belfrite.

The guard stands upright and shoulders broad. I

don't think I've ever seen a centaur in person. But if I ever saw one I'm sure he's it. Half man, Half Clydesdale horse. He makes his way towards us giving off some type of dark and negative vibe. Like I said warm welcome.

"State your purpose of travel." he says with a deep voice.

"Visitation of an old relative." I lie.

"We are fully booked. No more visitors for the week." he answers "You'll have to go somewhere else."

Why do I get the idea he's trying to be intimidating. He's in a bad mood I understand that but you can't just not let me in. I don't even have to answer these questions. Everyone knows that they have no true authority and they are just here for looks. If he is so grumpy, why can't he just let me in and not make things more difficult than need be? What should I do?

"Mar non lac te se lu," I state with a straight face. The centaur raises an eyebrow and takes half a step back. I've somehow managed to catch him off guard with that statement. He eyes me up and down. Like he's contemplating on whether what I said was true. A face that read "can it be true." He extends his hands to the gate and lets me in after he regains his composure.

The dark dungeon like doors open granting us access to the Trisector. I lightly whip the reigns to get the lizards to walk slowly. When the doors open it's like an entire city of itself. It's different since the last time I saw it. It still looks like the Trogonese war happened yesterday.

Wet mud sludging around on everyone's feet or shoes if they are rich enough to have any. The rain threatening to pierce through the cloth hand-made tiki huts. Which in Belfrite serves as homes and store structures. The poor people in this town. This is practically no man's land.

It's officially night time. The lightning the only thing illuminating the sky aside from the lit torches in the few shops still open. We'll have to check them out tomorrow. "Audrey," Trixie says "What did you say to him?"

"No idea." I said honestly "I just remember someone saying it when I was a kid. But don't worry about that right now. We need to hurry up and find shelter."

We continue onward through the streets of Belfrite in the Trisector. Children looking at us in awe because of the expensive lizard-drawn wagon. But I don't mind them for long. I have more important things to attend to. We trudge through all the milky dirt till we eventually get to a wooden post with two arrows on it. The one pointing to the right reads: the commons. The one pointing to the left reading: Beach. We head towards the beaches.

"Why are we headed to the beaches?" Trixie asks "There is a storm headed this way."

"Do you trust me?" I question.

She stares at me for a while and brings herself to nod in agreement.

We arrive at the beaches and drive towards the rocks. Eventually, I find the one I remember staying in as a kid. My grandfather showed me this place. I stayed here a bit earlier in my life. When I was still innocent. When I was still of the age where collecting seashells was the coolest thing ever and I wanted to open a store and sell seashell jewelry. But now, I'm back and am on a completely different journey.

We pull into the oversized rugged cave. The inside bigger than I remember. Well, it's dry and no one should find us here. Far down the beach is a huge tropical storm. Only if someone had a death wish. And even then they wouldn't need to come down here because they could just walk to a nearby shop and get the Moxus shot. We should be able to rest here undisturbed.

Trixie looks at me looking for confirmation. I just nod at her with a smile.

She climbs out of the stagecoach and begins to scan the cave. It's kinda wet but definitely uninhabited by any animals or bugs. Then again I'm sure even bugs and most animals don't know this place exist. Trixie balls up in a corner with a hint of a smile.

"Pass me that rock," I say.

She tosses it to me. And I strike the rope tying down

the luggage cases. I then toss the rock back to her. Proceeding to take down the luggage cases one by one. Trixie gets curious and decides to start opening them as I continue to pull them down.

The first one she reveals has bags filled with grain. I tell her to feed it to the lizards. The one I open has clothes in it. It's filled with dresses, skirts, and other feminine clothing. I hold the clothes up against my body. It brings out the color in my eyes and would fit me perfectly. It dwells on me slowly.

"You'd look so pretty in that" Trixie says looking at the shirt in my hands.

He really was coming to pick me up. After all the things he said. He was gonna buy me whether I liked it or not. He was just trying to seem polite about it. He's a smuggler, a criminal I remind myself. Of course, he lied. Somehow though my heart seems to still ache from the thought. Like I've gone through some type of betrayal. It doesn't matter I yell at myself. You've escaped now. That's not important.

Trixie and I finally get settled in. We change into warmer clothes we find in the suitcase. Then finish feeding our two new favorite lizards. I tell her how Lycrane liked to travel a lot and didn't always have money to do so. How I'd been to every region except Bolyen because of it. So after that bedtime story. We both headed to sleep.

‡   ‡   ‡

Chapter 6

Clunk, clunk, clunk. What's that sound? Morning already? No, I think, opening my eyes. *Clunk, clunk, clunk.* What is that? Oh my god! Are we moving? I sit up straight and reluctantly yawn.

The driver of our coach wagon looks back at me. Wearing a black cloak that resembles the one I use to own and an intricate mask disguising their face. The mask just staring at me. From the nose up it gives the impression of it being an actual face with painted swirls to emphasize the gold eyes. From the bridge of the nose down it's just a series of black and white swirls.

"Oh! You're awake," she says.

"Who are you and where is Trixie?" I say ignoring her statement.

"She's behind you. I guess she's still sleeping," she answers.

"Who are you and where are you taking us? How did

you even find us?"

"I was out looking for help. I also needed transportation. But somehow I found you two. You looked dehydrated and you didn't seem to have much so I just loaded you guys up on the stagecoach and decided to take you with me. It'd be nice to have some friends on my journey." she says happily.

"You totally ignored my first question but I'll let that slide." I said a tad aggravated "Where are you trekking to anyway?"

"We are headed to Crowel. Hopefully, we will be able to buy food and barter for other supplies while we are there."

"Crowel!" I say with shock "Your driving along the border of Zovoe and you want to go to Crowel for supplies. Why!" I say confused.

"Well, I like Crowel's shops and taverns. Plus we're almost there."

"What!" I scream "How long have we been sleeping?"

"Hmm. I'd say about three days." she says "Like I said you guys were quite dehydrated."

"It's Friday! You let us sleep that long?" I shout.

"Uh...yeah," she says, not sure of what to make of the situation. "Again. We're almost at Crowel."

When she says this clouds of mist start to depart and crumbled down castles are revealed. Bright green vines and moss running up and down the building sides. The Vytch's and creatures walking and trotting along the pebbled stone roads. A few guard dragons but that's to be expected for the mysterious town we know as Crowel.The nameless driver pulls forward into parking. The stagecoach hits a bit of a bump which wakes up Trixie.

We all get out of the stagecoach and Trixie and I try to wake ourselves. I catch her up on events and make sure to bring my new staff I'm so fond of. We all decide to split up and do a bit of shopping.

I just remind myself to stay out of sight. No need to draw extra attention and definitely no more serpents. I learned my lesson the first time. The message was well received. No more hazardous animal buying, ever. Just stick to berries and other foods.

Trixie doesn't look for anything, in particular, she just wanders. Our nameless driver seems to head to the pub and vanishes into its thick crowd. I casually just head over to a food stand. The merchant is talking to a customer so I don't really see their face. But whoever it may be they have done a wonderful job with their stand.

All the apples shiny, ripe, so it's all been freshly washed. The variety of berries all pre-packaged in special weaved baskets. This has to be the best fresh fruit stand I've ever laid my eyes on.

Even though Trixie and I woke up on our stolen stagecoach

with a nameless driver. It feels like things are finally starting to slow down. Maybe it's just me. Or maybe just being able to do a normal everyday task like grocery shopping is relieving stress. I exhale slowly taking everything in around me. It feels nice.

"Excuse me, can I help you with something?" the woman who runs the stand ask.

My eyes fly open "Oh, yes! How much is this basket of blueberries?"

"10 alfies." the merchant states.

Wow, that's so cheap I think to myself. There must be like 4 pounds of blueberries in that nicely woven basket. I think I'm in love with Crowel. Seems to give you a bang for your buck. Speaking of bucks...how much money do I have? I haven't needed to buy anything since that day in La Bobo Cree.

I pull out a single bead forgetting that it's changed back to its original form. No matter I'll just change it back. I finish the transaction and the merchant closes her drop box. That's when something catches my eyes. A seemingly neverending line out the door from a tiki hut next door. What could that line be for? Is someone giving out free gold? "Ah, I see the shop next door has caught your eye." the merchant says sadly.

"Yeah."

"It's sad really. People day in and day out lining up for that shot. Feeling like they have nothing to live for. But I can't complain too much. I serve them their last meals. Don't get me wrong. What's good for this business isn't always good for the heart. It kills me to watch the line next door dwindle. But I have my own family to worry about."

Trixie then stumbles into me from running too fast. She grabs onto my shirt digging both of her hands into it. Looking up at me with eyes full of panic. While still gasping for air a bit.

"The nameless driver... I finally...got...her name. It's Lennox. Anyway, we have to get her." Trixie pants.

"What about her? What happened?" I ask.

"She's a sloppy drunk. She's gonna draw too much attention."

"Well, where is she?" I ask her.

Clank, bang, ping.

"Nevermind, I think I found her."

Trixie and I rush towards the direction of the sound. All we find is the nameless driver. I mean Lennox stumbling and staggering around outside of the pub. Knocking over pots and pans from nearby stands. She even knocks over customers who just came out with their bags from the store. Lennox, what are you doing? This wasn't part of the plan at all. What were you thinking?

Trixie runs to her side and tries to prop her up. When Trixie almost has Lennox in a position where she can support herself. Lennox's mask slides off her face and hits the ground. Trixie bends over to pick it up. I pick up my pace so I can hold Lennox in the mean time.

A vytch screams "Lennox! Is that you? You owe me money!"

It seems that this resonates with everyone in town considering that they all turn to stare at us. What is happening? What did she do? Is this what she wanted us to help her with! She should've warned us. How can we help with what we don't know about?

Another Vytch screams "I'm gonna collect the bounty on your head!"

"Vevro set the price at a hundred thousand alfies."

"Damn it," I whisper to myself under my breath.

They start to approach us. I back away slowly with Lennox in my arms. These remarks seem to have her sobering up though. How do you handle a situation like this? What can you do? Think Audrey, think. They're closing in on you. Think a bit faster.

Trixie looks at me with eyes saying make the call. Come on Audrey. You escaped slavery you can totally figure something out.

So I make the call. We all turn around and run as fast as possible. Cutting through the crowd like our lives depend on it. Mostly because our lives might actually depend on it. We aren't 100 percent sure where we are headed. As long as it's away from them we could be running in circles for all I care. This moment feels familiar. Like it was just yesterday. Except for the last time this happened, it wasn't a town full of people chasing me with their torches screaming bloody murder. They aren't even after me. They are after Lennox. She reminds me so much of Lycrane. Getting themselves into trouble with no safe way out.

I don't know how but Lennox seems to be completely sober now. We literally are running side by side. Trixie is actually ahead of us. At least I know she won't be trampled by the angry mob ready to kill us. With them being Vytches and what not if they catch us at least I won't have to worry about them burning us at the stake. Maybe they'll suck are blood till we are empty. But I prefer the second one. Not being burned alive. Or being tied to a chair and drowned for that matter. So there are some pluses.

The angry mob roars louder. We all head down the road with trees arching over it. Only fragments of lights making their way down through all the tree leaves and branches every so often. The road is also lined with tombstones and flowers. Some have crosses, others have angels praying. We could use an angel right now.

Lennox and I finally catch up to Trixie and we are all

running side by side. Finally having put some distance between us and the mob. *Boom.* I hit my head. Lennox pushes me off of her. Trixie rolls over. I rub my head wondering what is happening. I blink a few times trying to correct my vision. What was I hit by just now? My ribcage is feeling a bit bruised. Ow.

"WHAT THE H-." a random girl muffles Lennox's mouth and raises her pointer finger to her rose pink lips.

Everyone huddles closer together. Hiding behind a big smooth tombstone. Which is a few inches away from a ruin. The angry townspeople run by us. Not hearing or spotting us. I asked for an angel and apparently, I got one. Lennox slaps the mysterious girl's hand away. She is upset and red in the face.

"That's not nice Lennox. She just saved our lives." Trixie says.

"Yeah by the way who are you?"

"No time to explain." the girl says with dirt patches scattered across her face. "I just need you to trust me. We both know that your not ordinary travelers. I don't know what brought you here. I don't care. I'm just going with my gut feeling on this. Either way, my job is to help you. I can't really explain it. But I know someone who might."

"Wait! You just come and tackle us out of nowhere. With no reasonable explanation and just expect us to trust you?

You're kidding." Lennox argues.

"Again she just saved us." Trixie points out.
"I'm not going." Lennox pouts.

"Fine. Stay here and wait for that angry mob to come back and eat you alive." the girl in the post-apocalyptic outfit answers.
"Eatin' alive." Lennox says as blood drains from her face

"Alright. I'll come along. Don't expect me to be happy about it though."
"Of course not." I say "Why would you be."

We all get up and dust ourselves off. Removing pebbles, dirt, and even bugs off our clothes. When we all catch our breath the mysterious girl leads us in the direction from the side she had tackled us from. It seems that we are following a hidden river upstream. I can hear it but I still can't see much. Since we are off the path now everything has gotten even darker. A few steps later my pant leg gets slushed in water. Where are we headed that we went from river to marsh.
"This better not be a trick." Lennox threatens.

"Would you give it a rest already," Trixie says. Who knew Trixie had a bit of sass in her. We keep running and the trees eventually start to peel away. Light slowly begins to unveil a small cottage in the distance. And the marsh covered ground turns into a bright green hill. What a beautiful cottage.

Arriving at the cottage we see a small old lady with stunning gray hair wearing a floral apron. Standing over a bowl filled with still bottled water. The potion bottles and cauldrons and a bunch of other witch working tools behind her on wooden shelves. Everything is surprisingly organized. I was expecting more cobwebs and dust. "Grandma these must be the travelers. I told you I had a gut feeling. There here."

The grandmother stares down into her bowl. Not a hundred percent sure of everything she's being told. She takes a fig branch and stirs the water until it has a little whirlpool. We all just stand there in silence.
The wind blows a cold gust through the window making the curtains dance. The windchimes start making beautiful music. The grandma looks at all of us with a smile.

"Yes, I thought I saw your faces in my scrying bowl. I was expecting you. Just not this soon. Usually, I see things weeks ahead of time. I only saw you three yesterday. No matter, right now we must head to the shore. Good job Jessica. Your intuition is getting better." she removes her apron and we all head out.

‡   ‡   ‡

Chapter 7

We all reach the white sandy beach. Nothing but dark blue oceans for miles. Waves washing in and out slowly. The old lady gathers us around in a circle and tells us to listen closely. Out of the three of us, we aren't sure what to expect next. No one has a clue of what she or anyone for that matter could say next. It's like every word and every action is something that would change our lives forever.

"What the hell is that!" Lennox screams at the top of her lungs pointing down the shore.
We all look and see bodies lined up to the left of where we stand. All genders of all species. Some clothes some not. Lined up side by side. Skin pale and motionless. Dead...they're all dead. Shock and horror on our faces.

"Are you trying to kill us you ole Vytch!"
"No, I swear I'm just here to help." she says defensively.

"Explain it then. Explain that to me," she yells.

Jessica, the apocalyptic girl says "Shhhh. She's not gonna kill you. Please keep your voices down. The townspeople will hear you and come this way. We'll lose valuable time."

"Then you better give me a damn good explanation," Lennox says through gritted teeth.

"Okay Okay." the grandmother says "Listen. Not all the Vytches in Crowel are nice people." she starts.

"That's an understatement," Lennox says rolling her eyes.

"Some make a game of taking lost travelers and make them go through a series of puzzles just to draw them all the way out here. Just so they can drink their blood. But I promise I won't do that to you. We must hurry. Please just trust me. We are wasting time."

"I don't trust her," Lennox says with a straight face.

Trixie says "Well I do and I think Audrey does as well. So please let her finish."

"Thankyou." the grandmother smiles "So this is what happens. I am going to do a sacred Vytch ritual. This ritual takes you and transports your soul to Bolyen."

"Our soul!" Lennox says.

"Lennox shut up," Trixie shouts.

"Listen this ritual won't work if everybody is angry. You must be calm before you do this type of ritual."

"Let's get this done with already." Trixie states "Just let me go through the ritual first or we'll be here all day." The small old lady stands behind Trixie and looks me in the eye.

"Trixie." I say firmly "Are you sure you want to do this? It's risky."

She gives me a slight smile "You said you wouldn't let anything bad happen to me. Right? So I'm fine."

I give her a smile in return. There she goes again. Being a silly kid while being an adult all at the same time. She never fails to amaze me.

As I think this the grandmother opens her mouth wide and pierces Trixie's neck with her sharp fangs. A little bit of blood runs out the side. She swishes some of the blood in her mouth from left to right. You'd think it was Listerine. She spits it out and as it travels across the sky and over the ocean it dissolves and disappears.

"What did you just do?!" I scream.

"Her soul has traveled to Bolyen."

"I'm not going to Bolyen. Watching that was disgusting. You're not going to do that to m-" she bites Lennox.

"Thankyou. I thought I was going to have a fight with her." I say "Also before I go. I also wanted to say that. If everything turns out well. I'll come back and be able to thank you

70

properly."

"I'd like that. Oh and before I forget. When you arrive at Bolyen. Find the leader and tell her that White Lotus sent you." she says making sure to emphasize every part.
She bites me after that and everything is dark. My eyes have become heavy and I can only feel and hear. Her fangs hitting my veins like hot iron. Scorching them alive. My own blood slowly sliding down my neck raising the hairs on my neck leaving goosebumps. People are screaming. They sound so angry. I can't tell where it's coming from. I feel scared but then I feel light. Like I'm flying. Not like a feather or spit like I saw earlier when she did the ritual for Trixie. It feels like I am light itself.

‡   ‡   ‡

Chapter 8

I feel myself getting heavier. The weight firmly settling. Blue everything is blue, cold, and wet. I'm submerged in blue. Where am I? Why do I feel so strange.

"Audrey!" I hear a voice "Audrey!"
I sit up and cough up water that seems to have filled my lungs. Which burns my insides. Then it all just randomly stops. Weird, It's like I'm able to breathe water. How does one simply upchuck and then seconds later be able to breathe it all in?

"Audrey, are you okay?"
I'm finally able to open my eyes. They just fly open and I'm greeted by Trixie's face. She's just staring down at me she's blurry. Unfocused. Gold blobs surrounding her. So this is how people feel when they teleport places. Nauseous, confused, and half alive.

"I'm fine." I murmur as everything starts to stable itself.

"Good." she says with a grin on her face.

"Where are we?"

"Bolyen. We actually made it. We actually traveled to the underwater city of spirits." she says excitedly.

"I can breathe water," I say.

"Our tangible bodies are still on shore. Right now you are just a soul. You felt bad because you were still adjusting." a lady says with black silk hair pulled back into a bubble ponytail.

"And who are you?" I say.

"It's Lennox silly." Trixie says "She looks really pretty without her mask and when she's not drinking herself to death."

Lennox ignores the statement "So where to now?"

"The leader. We must find him. Or her." I say standing up with my staff in my right hand.

I scan our surroundings. We seem to be standing on the doorstep of a humungous spherical air dome. Beads falling down around the perimeter. A rainbow fish with a slash of illegible characters swims up to us. Staring and analyzing. We just wait.

Finally, he goes "Can I help you guys with something?"

"Um...you might?" Trixie starts.

"We are looking for the leader. We're new here." I say.

"Obviously." he goes in a belittling tone "You're literally standing on the steps of the throne. I don't know what you're up to. But if you try something she'll kick you back out here. I'll deal with you then." the rainbow fish states then swims off.

"Well, that was a warm welcome," Trixie says.

"To say the least." Lennox finishes.

We turn around noticing the big double doors in front of us. They don't automatically open or slide. There are no door handles. Just a door.

"Any ideas?" Lennox inquires.

"Well..." I start.

"We can't go around it," Trixie says.

"We can't go under it." Lennox says as we all watch a whale cross under us.

"And we can't go over it. So we must go..." I say poking the door sending ripples throughout the makeup of the door "Through it,"

We all walk through the door ending up in exactly what the rainbow fish called it. A throne. Chandeliers of gold light running throughout the open floor layout. Swordfish standing at their post. Oddly enough there's a puffer fish running a well-kept bar nearby to our left. It's also surprisingly warm in here. Because I thought fish were cold-blooded creatures. Directly in front of me though. Is a set of stairs made of water leading up to a silver steel chair made up of pink coral and white pearls…and empty.

"Excuse me," I say, words echoing throughout the hall.

All the swordfish turn towards us.

"We need to speak to the leader."

A woman with magenta eyes, rose lips, and long black wavy hair stops mid-step. She's wearing a white Egyptian toga dress. Her ivory skin tone glowing. Raising her hand to the bridge of her nose then whispering something to herself.

"So many interruptions today." she says clearly.

"We need to speak to someone in authority sometime this week," Lennox states rudely.

The swordfish give us an evil eye as to remind us of who we're speaking to.

"White Lotus sent us," I say firmly hoping that it helps our situation.

The woman looks up at us. Her eyes fixate on me. Her facial expression softens.

"I am Mira. That beautiful chair up there belongs to me. What may I help you with?" she says softly and shyly.

"Well we needed a place to crash." says Lennox.

"Yeah, we just finished getting chased by the townspeople of Crowel," Trixie adds.

Mira's eyes break away from mine. Slowly falling onto my staff.

"You are welcome to stay with me. A friend of white lotus is a friend of mine." she says warmly "Make yourself at home. But first, i'd like to talk to the one holding the staff."

"My name is Audrey." I introduce myself starting to approach her.

"Yes, Audrey. May I talk to you privately," she says shaking my hands.

"I don't see why not," I reply.

"Very well. This way please," she says as she shoos me down a nearby corridor past the bar.

Mira and I walk past a few doors. All completely made of pink pearls. Everything is seemingly upbeat and welcoming. But I'm starting to feel like Lennox. Should I really be so easy to trust these people. They are absolute strangers to me. Mira could secretly feed me to her pet shark if she wanted to. Just because she can.

Stopping in our tracks Mira opens a door on the left side of the hall. The room is more casual than the throne room. The wall has coral running among the walls as if it's some professionally designed wallpaper. A fish tank on the left side of the room. A silver table in the middle with some fish wrapped snacks. Two bubble shaped white leathery hover chairs on either side.

Mira looks at me and smiles "Will you join me for lunch?"

"Of course," I say politely.

We both enter the room, Mira, closing the door behind us. Her expression turns more serious. Her body language changes. Almost as if she's not trying to be proper anymore. No longer trying to maintain appearances. I take my seat anyway despite the change of mood. Mira sits across from me. She unwraps a pre-packaged fish wrapped snack. Time passes.

Finally, she says "Do you know about the Alfralon religion?"

"Yes, I believe in the Alfralon religion. To be humble, kind, and keep the greater picture and others well being in mind." I tell Mira.

"Do you know how it all began?" Mira questions.

"No." I stutter a bit embarrassed.

"It's nothing to be embarrassed about Audrey. I don't think any living person knows what I'm about to tell you."

I raise and eyebrow. What did she really bring me here for?

"First, I will tell you about the origins of our religion which we hold dear. Second, I will tell you the origins of the staff you hold that you seem to be very fond of. If you weren't it wouldn't have come with you to Bolyen." she says seriously "You must never tell anyone these things. After all, somethings are meant to only be known among the dead."

"I swear, you have my word," I promise.

"In the beginning, there were three gods."

"Baron, Eivor, and Indigo."

"Exactly." she said "They weren't sure of how to...proceed in their new found roles. I mean the first gods in all of history. There was no manual or instruction on how to be a god. They only knew of the power and responsibility. They only knew that their job was to watch over the people who lived their day to day lives. Watch the inhabitants of Xyron. Drinking wine, eating fresh fruits, and being happy."

"So what happened? How is this different than what we believe to be true today?" I interrupt.

"Baron, the overseer of the harvest...healer of population...and majority of magic. He got in a terrible fight with the goddess Indigo."

"The happy God?"

"Yes. Indigo the goddess of the war and hunting, protection, water, and people who hold the ability to prophesize."

"Wait Indigo oversees war. She's the happy one?" I

say confused.

"It helps to have a happy goddess oversee war. It means less wars and fights among the people. If you're happy all the time. You wouldn't impulsively start a war," she says looking away from me now.

"Until..." I urge her to continue the story.

"Until Baron and Indigo's fight got so intense. That it started our last war." she says seemingly a bit upset. Almost as if she is reliving a memory first hand.

"The Trogonese war," I stated frowning a bit.

"The war had started. But the gods were so busy fighting that they didn't take note of it. Instead the goddess Eivor. Overseer of wisdom. Recommended that since everyone was new at this that they should all calm down and just get to know each other. That Xyron was running smoothly so far so no one would notice."

"And since no one noticed the Trogonese war. It just carried itself out. Until everyone just stopped fighting. Centuries later." I followed up.

"Correct." said Mira.

"But what about my staff?"

"Their last act." Mira says in a noble and honorable tone

"They decided that they would build a key. A significant, unheard of, key artifact. The Solar Eclipse. They used their key elements and crafted the beautiful staff you hold here before me. Designed to only be found when the world is in complete darkness. When claimed it is supposed to send a signal up to the gods alerting them that they were once again needed. In the meantime, the hero would rise and buy time while they came up with a plan."

"But nothing is happening. They don't seem to be doing anything."

"I know." Mira says "We the people of Bolyen have come to the conclusion...that since they've been on a break for about let's say 300 years. Assuming they really did try to bond the first 100 years and come up with a protocol and or plan. That since we didn't need them all that time. That we don't need them now. That it will just play out. Like a permanent state of procrastination."

"People like me. Believers of the Alfralon religion. We solely believe in empowering ourselves. Doing as much as we can to be a good person. Be humble and kind. And trying to only pray when in desperate need of a miracle. We aren't exactly hassling them. By shouting our prayers, wishes, and desires on them."

"Yeah," Mira says calmly.

"Wait a minute!" I shout "You mean I'm supposed to do this by myself. No help from the gods. I barely can wield magic. I can do one illusion trick. ONE."

"You came here with friends. They will help."

"I hope so," I whisper to myself.

"We should get back." she says getting out of her leathery white bubble shaped hover chair.

I get up as well.

‡   ‡   ‡

Chapter 9

Mira and I proceed back down the corridors through which we came. I always thought being a leader there would be more security around me personally. Watching every move I make. But that doesn't seem to be the case with Mira and her guardsman. Maybe I should stop believing everything I hear.

We reach the throne hall. I freeze where I stand in the middle of the walkway. My feet are made of cement blocks. I can't move my feet. I'm shaking rhythmlessly. I'm burning up. This can't be happening. Whatever this maybe? My mouth is dry and chapped. I'm not able to speak or scream and yell for help. Trixie. . .what happened to you?
Her body mysteriously levitating by the staircase. A soft purple light glowing from her body. Isn't she human? She's not supposed to glow strange colors or levitate.

Her eyes closed and her long waist length platinum

blonde hair hitting the floor. It's like she's laying down on an invisible bed. In a dream state. More like a nightmare. Her body is starting to thrash. She's scaring me to death. Trixie begins to foam at the mouth a bit.

Mira screams for a doctor or any type of medical assistance. I finally muster up the strength to move. Though it does still feel like I have a ball and chain on me. I run to her side. I can't move her. What if I accidentally hurt her? Her fingers are trembling relentlessly. Toes continuing to curl then uncurl themselves. Is she in pain?

A medical assistant finally comes and I notice they have no equipment what so ever. How do they expect to help? Without tools, you're just as good as anyone else here. Mira stands steadily behind me. Where is Lennox in all this chaos? I hope she's alright. I have enough to worry about with Trixie in this state. I turn to Mira.

"What did your guards do to her?" I accuse.

"I swear I didn't do anything." she exclaims.

"She was fine before we got here. She was healthy as a horse."

"Is that so?" says the medical assistant.

"Yeah," I assure him.

"How old is she?" he asked in a deep voice.

"Well, I believe she is around 10. If not exactly." I state.

"I think I know the problem then?"

"What is it?" Mira asks with genuine concern.
"She's dying."

"Well, we know that already," Lennox says as she stumbles into the throne room.
"I was takin' a piss." she says slurred.

"Excuse her language." I tell Mira "She's most likely been drinking from your bar."
"I see." she says staying calm.

"So go ahead doc. Tell us something we don't know." Lennox yells.
"Lennox this is serious!" I say.

"You always were a big crybaby. A worry wart then. A worry wart now. When are you gonna grow up?" she says still falling all over the place.
"I have no idea what you're talking about. Just stay out of the way."

"Yes, mom."
I turn back to the medical assistant looking for answers. Tell me you can fix this. She'll be fine right. She won't die on us. She'll be able to do everything she wanted to do. She can't die. We just escaped from slavery. Trixie hasn't had a chance to have a normal life yet. Please tell me good news. I think to myself trying to not break into tears.

"Like I said she's dying."

"Can you elaborate on that doctor?" Mira says through gritted teeth getting impatient.

"From what I've been told you guys aren't officially dead yet. You came under different circumstances."

"Yes, that's correct."

"So...from what I've gathered. Your souls are still maintaining some type of connection with your bodies. Which I assume is still on the shores of Crowel. Think of it this way. Her soul is drowning. She's probably been out of her body too long. Her body can't handle it." the medical assistant explains.

"But I'm fine." I point out.

"But you're older. Your body and soul are more fully developed than a 10-year-old gi-."

A scream comes from behind all of us. A banshee wail threatening to burst any and every eardrum throughout the planet Xyron. A woman runs towards us and falls to her knees beside me. Her light brown wavy hair drenching her face. A few strands flying away. Who does she think she is? What's with the sudden interruption? Why did she scream? Mira calls the guards on her with a snap of her fingers. Within seconds the swordfish come to take her away. When the first guard lays a finger on her she slaps it away. Another guard grabs her by the arms picking her up off the ground. The woman starts kicking in her toga dress. Her face turns red as she fights off the guards.

"Unhand me." she screams "That's my daughter over there." she cries "That's my daughter." she sobs.
"Let her go," I say having no authority.

Mira nods in consent.
The guards drop the woman letting her fall to her knees. They all fall back into their original standing post. We all resume panic over Trixie. Though my head is a bit cloudy from the woman's outburst. Is she really her mother? Now that I can get a better look at her she does share some of the same features as Trixie. The long hair, pouty pink lips, and the slim nose and smooth skin.

"So can you help her?" the woman says to the medical assistant with eyes full of tears.
"No, I can't." he says bluntly.

She stands in a rage "I'm supposed to sit here and watch my daughter die! What kind of doctor are you?"
"I'm a doctor." he states "Not a miracle worker."

Mira interrupts "Katherine…you never told me you had children." she says with a hint of sorrow in her voice.
"Because I was embarrassed. When I was alive. I did horrible things. Things I'm not proud of. I don't like to talk about it." She admits.

"It's ok Katherine," Mira says lending her comfort. "All we can do is wait for the little one to wake up."

"Alright," Mira says.

"When and *if* she does. I will run test on her then. I will also be asking her some questions." he finishes.

"Thank you," Mira responds.

Katherine grabs Trixie's hand. Looking up at Trixie's floating body. Once again it's become motionless. I look at Katherine look at Trixie. She's hurting on the inside. I can't imagine what she's feeling. It must feel worst than what I was feeling the first time I escaped without Trixie.

"You really love her don't you?" I whisper.

"Of course I do. She's my daughter," she says sweetly.

"Yeah," I say exhaling.

"What was she even doing down here? She can't be dead. She's only 10." she says.

"Well." I say hesitantly "I escaped slavery. When I did I took her with me. She was so nice and smart. I couldn't bare to just leave her there. She deserved better."

"Wow, you've already been a better parent to her than I have. I lost her due to my own dumb gambling addiction. I was so stupid. I bet she hates me." she laughs in sadness.

"Not at all." I tell Katherine "She's actually been really happy since the day I met her. She was singing Bobo Lani when we first ran into each other. She never complained about the type of hard working labor we did either. She's only 10. But I think she forgave you a long time ago."

87

Katherine laughs raising a hand to her mouth "She still sings that. I use to sing that to her every night as a little girl. I can't believe she still remembers all of that. That's good to hear. I can't wait for her to wake up. I want to hear her voice. I want to get to know her. See what I've missed since I lost her. Since I inconveniently died before finding her."

"You were looking for her?" I ask.

"Of course. I did everything I could to get her back. I wanted to find her." she says "Then when I finally did after all these years." she sighs with a disapproving tone "This is what I found. A levitating yet motionless body."

"You know I think she'd be extremely happy to know that you were out there somewhere trying as hard as you can to spend time with her. I think any kid would. Especially Trixie." I state.

"You think so."

"I know so."

I'm trying my hardest not to beat myself up. I'm not sure why or how. Not completely sure when it happened. But I like Trixie. I relate to her. She's like. . . I guess a daughter to me. I can't explain it. I just feel it. Could it be that I'm jealous? The pain I'm experiencing the palpitation of my heart from forcing myself to create a comfortable conversing with a woman who claims to be her mother. Some woman who just shows up at the most inconvenient time in my opinion. Sure she was dead now. But maybe she should've tried harder! Maybe she shouldn't have lost Trixie in the first place! I scream in my head for the world to hear.

Audrey get ahold of yourself. Trixie isn't yours. I think as I try to calm myself down to a more relaxed state of mind. She's not yours and she's not you. Plus it's up to Trixie if she wants to stay with Katherine or leave with you. This is Trixie's decision.

Not to mention Trixie may not even recognize this woman. Trixie might have forgiven her as a person. But does Trixie recognize her mom as a motherly figure in her life still. After all, Katherine didn't get to do much parenting in the early years of her life.

I exhale lightly. Relinquishing any and all of the anger and jealousy my body might be trying to hold onto. I need to be tranquil. I shouldn't be losing my head over things like this. It's a big deal that Katherine is here. But I am still supposed to be at Trixie's side. My focus should be on the here and now. Not the aftermath of her waking up. Katherine looks at me with wondering eyes as if to ask was I alright. I don't answer. I just rise from my knees while looking at the floor. Deciding to make my way to the bar for a drink. How can I comfort Katherine or pray for Trixie if being in the same proximity of them simultaneously makes me lose my wits. I can't think clearly like this. If I'm no use to either of them, might as well have a drink. Plus it could be a long time before she wakes up.

When I reach the bar I lay my hands and arms flat on the counter top. The Bapus bartender cleaning out a martini glass with a towel. Then proceeding to make me a martini without my say so. I'm not gonna question anything. Just gonna sit here and enjoy my drink. Nothing wrong with a little alcohol. I take a sip of the martini savoring the horrendous taste of liquor. It's like someone took all the bad things in life. All the sins. Ground it up together and juiced it.

Yet here I am enjoying every bit of it. Is that why you liked it so much, grandpa? Because it tasted like everyone's sin. Is that how it works? It reminds you of how good of a person you are, by giving you something to compare it to? Giving the good and bad a measurability that everyone can understand. Everyone agrees upon. Cause whether we admit it or not. Everyone drinks.

Everyone drinks and we all do it willingly. No one to force or pressure us. Just ourselves, a bottle, and a glass. We take it and pour ourselves a glass. Pull up a seat. Then enjoy the sins of others. It's like a secret passageway to building a god like complex. Not forever, but just a moment.

A moment all too soon Katherine pulls up a seat next to me. Can't she see I need some space. I'm trying to be subtle about the distance we have. So I don't make any commentary. Keep drinking and don't make eye contact. She's staring at me again I can feel it. Her eyes are piercing me.

"You don't look like the drinking type." she says.

"Maybe because I'm not. Maybe because underneath it all, I am. Though I don't like to admit it so I hide it. Who knows?" I say as I circle my glass in the air by waving my wrist.

"So childhood trauma."

I don't give her any confirmation or show any denial about her conclusion.

"Well hey, we've all been there. We all have our demons kid," she says acting all too casually.

I gesture the nearby bartender to issue me another drink still trying to ignore her efforts of making a conversation. Frankly, I think I've dealt with my past. I don't need her help to relive it. I don't need anyone's help dwelling or pretending that "oh, I've come so far since then" attitude. I just want to leave it behind me. Dead and buried in the ground.

"Listen, I know what you're going through. I've been there. My parents were on drugs most of my life. I ruined Trixie's with my gambling issues. That's just the icing on the cake. So if anyone knows what the definition of trauma is it's me. If it's demons and obstacles and being lower than low. I know. Because I've done it all. Every sin the gods that may or may not be above us could strike me down for if I was still alive."

"Get to the point. What are you a motivational speaker? You're just droning on and on without telling me anything of actual value." I say getting impatient with her. The bartender puts down my fresh drink in front of me.

Katherine doesn't hesitate to intentionally knock it over. The glass rolls on the counter. The drink itself forming a puddle on the table. It makes its way to the edges and starts dripping off the edge of the counter. Katherine gets up from the stool.
"That's enough for you." she says trying to contain her anger before storming off.

Hours passed by after that in complete silence. Occasionally there was loud pacing because Katherine was growing impatient. It's really eating her alive. I just remain at the bar continuously throwing back drinks. Not caring what kind or how many. I'm surprised I'm not drunk yet though. I guess reality can keep you sober like that. Worrying over people you care about will keep you sober like that.

I sense movement by the staircase. I quickly whip my head around to see it's Trixie waking up. Katherine runs and grabs Trixie in an embrace, beating me to her. Squeezing her till she almost pops, as if the girl didn't just almost die. Trixie coughs up water and other fluids on Katherine in response. Can't say I didn't enjoy that a bit. Katherine still doesn't let go.

Trixie looks up "Mom?" she says confused.

"Yes, it's me."

I just stand there pissed at Katherine but relieved that Trixie is ok. All the color has returned to her face. She seems healthy. You'd think she wasn't feeling sick that entire time. So if she wasn't feeling pain all that time, what did she feel? What really happened?

"Are you feeling alright" Katherine beats me to the punch again.

"Yes, I'm fine."

"Do you feel any different? Do you want something to drink?" Katherine keeps bantering her.

Trixie ignores her and comes to hug me. Aw, I feel special.

"What was that for?" I ask.

"You looked worried."

I answer "Yeah, you gave us quite the scare. Do yo-"

"Need anything?" Katherine interrupts again.

"Would you stop breathing down her throat?" I say.

"Yeah mom, I'm fine," Trixie says.

"Sorry I just want to spend time with my daughter." she says.

"Still give her some space," I say letting myself get angry.

Lennox comes up behind me feeling my frustration. Trixie moves from in between us. We're probably getting too loud. But the swordfish don't say anything. They just give us a watchful eye.

"Plus, what do you know about parenting. You're just a kid."

The staff starts glowing on and off repeatedly. Glowing a bright teal. I don't make much of it or let it concern me because I'm too busy arguing with Katherine. It's just a glowing orb after all. It's old and stuff. It could be just giving out. Only the Alfralon gods would know.

"Cause your just so motherly," I say theatrically.

"You don't know what I had to go through." she spits.

"Same here, so stop acting like you know me. Stop acting like you can relate." I point out.

Lennox gets in between us. She starts trying to haul me back. Trixie grabs onto my shirt. The staff starts glowing more rapidly. Then everything is white.

‡   ‡   ‡

Chapter 10

"Where are we?" I say " I can't see a thing. Everything is a white blob?" I state.

"I don't know? I can't see anything either," she states. "WHY IS EVERYTHING WHITE!" Lennox screams at the top of her lungs "OH MY GOD ARE WE BLIND?!"

"We're not blind. Everybody just calm down." I say. "You guys it's ok." Trixie states "I can see now. It wears off."

Minutes later we all have our vision back. We find ourselves deep in snow. Explains why there was a sudden chill. There are stores made of stone on both sides of us. A bus stop next to us with a time stamp. It reads: April 30th, 2904 time 6:45 pm.

"Trixie," I say trying to get her attention.

"Yes." she responds.

"I'm sorry that this all happened. I'm sure you would have

rathered stayed with your mom. Probably wanting to get to know her and what not."

"Are you kidding? I love my mom but I would never give up this amazing adventure. It's awesome." she states excitedly.

"Excuse me." Lennox intervenes "Is no one concerned that your stupid staff just teleported us to God knows where? We were souls outside of bodies. That could've went terribly wrong! One of us could've died!" she says full of concern.

"I doubt it." I say casually "Mira told me the history of this 'stupid staff' she said it was created by the Alfralon gods."

"Pfft. You believe that bull."

"As you just pointed out. It re-connected our souls to our bodies then here. It would have to be pretty powerful to do that."

"Well aren't you at least concerned that we are lost?" she asks me.

"We're not lost." I point in the direction of the road "That's the tower that the council lives in." I say.

Trixie continues "We're far from lost. We're finally close to Audrey's destination. This is where she's been headed all along. I'm just tagging along for fun."

"So should we start walking. If we walk now we should get there before they call a quits for today."

"Yeah, more adventures."

"I don't want to walk," Lennox complains.

"You can get a room for the night. We're in the center of Bagoa after all."

Her head drops to her chest. Frustration and sadness simultaneously taking over her.

"What's wrong?" Trixie questions.

"I don't have any money."

"So walking it is. Let's get a move on people. We're wasting valuable time. Plus we're almost there." I say excitedly taking in the fact that we are actually in Zovoe. We finally made it.

We tread towards the skyscraping tower in the distance with 6-inch snow covering our feets. The glowing crescent moon rising higher in the sky with every footstep. I wonder if the Alfralon gods are watching us march to our future victory. The wind begins to howl. It's like a blizzard is coming our way.

"I'm so cold," Lennox complains.

When we finally do arrive at the council's tower standing over 8 stories tall. After all the walking and continuous stops. All the complaining from Lennox and dog whimpers from the dark corners of alleyways from stray cats cold and hungry. The door before me in all its glory. I adore it as if it was made of pure gold. Beautiful polished sparkling gold. The doorsteps are under our feet. I savor the moment and the feeling of accomplishment. It's so beautiful. We finally decide to open the door to realize it's a small elevator. It has bright red carpet. Skylights. And white panels. It's the nicest elevator ever invented. We step inside and we all let out a deep sigh. Allowing ourselves to relax and enjoy the escape from the newly falling snow.

"At least it's warm," Lennox says.
"Just shut up already, you're bringing back bad memories," I say.

We hit the up button and take off to our destiny.

‡   ‡   ‡

Chapter 11

Arriving at the top floor, the elevator opens. Seeing 4 empty navy blue leather chairs left in darkness. The moon shining so brightly through the windows behind them they're practically black silhouettes. Their shadows reaching to our feet. We step out the elevator.

We step out and realize we missed the obvious. A huge breathtaking red dragon sits to the right of the chairs. His head down and eyes rested. Calmly the dragon breathes in and out. It must be asleep. Or pretending to be. "That's some heavy security. Who keeps a dragon in the front room?" Lennox asks.

We're approached by a young guy with white hair and a long flowing amethyst-colored cape. Is he on the council? Of course, he is. But is he the head of council? He stands in front of me with cardboard boxes stacked on top of one another. He places them to the side on the floor.

"OH! We have visitors. Hi. I'm Xyron, the male head of council. Can I help you?" he says.

"Um...I'm Audrey. This is Trixie and Lennox." I say introducing all of us "We came because we had some serious concerns about the living standards and businesses throughout Xyron."

"Well, This is an unheard of occasion. I can't wait to hear your concerns. Hopefully, we can find a solution to these problems and concerns. After all, we all want what is best for Xyron. But as you can see we are out at the moment. Even the council needs sleep. So tomorrow will be your hearing. The council will let you present your concerns and possible solutions if any and see what we can do." he finishes.

"What? Wait! What are we suppose to do right now? Do you expect us to go back out there and freeze to death?" Lennox says angrily.

"On the contrary," he says nobly "There are plenty of empty rooms here for you to stay in. Spend the night here in the tower. I assume that will take care of your sleeping and eating arrangements to your comfort."

With that being said Lennox and Trixie end up branching off to find the rooms down the left hall. I stay not really wanting to go to the rooms yet.

"If you're not tired. We also have a library and gym," he states.

"A library? Where?" I ask.

"It's down the right corridor. Keep walking till you see the blue-tinted sliding doors. You can't miss it." he instructs.

"Thank you," I say.

"No problem. If you'll excuse me then I have boxes I need to store away," he says picking up the boxes and heading off.

I followed his instructions precisely and I completely understand now why he said I couldn't miss it. You wouldn't be able to tell from the exterior of the building. But the library is like it's own separate wing. It's almost 3 stories tall. Which must mean we are way more than 8 stories above ground. This library is a beautiful illusion.

It's perfect from the filing of books to the freshly kept shelves that hold them. The soft and mellow scent of vanilla hinted in the air. The lights at a comfortable setting that way it doesn't blind you or too low of having to squint when you read small words in the books. They even have holographic books. Which I didn't even know was a thing. This is the council's tower though so I guess some of the things here aren't exactly for the public eye. But lucky me, Xyron gave me permission. He did say make myself at home.

I make the decision to find a book on the less known magical incidents on magic. Hoping I would find a book that would explain to me why Trixie went into her levitating fit so suddenly or why I received a turquoise mark on my right arm in the shape of a straight line when we left Bolyen. Someone somewhere in all of Xyron history must have had a similar experience. Someone had to have recorded something like that. I mean it can't be a complete freak accident.

I scour through the books just looking for some type of dusty record or file on these unheard of events. Two librarians spotted me but didn't pay me enough mind to ask if I needed help or not. When I reach for a book finding what might be just what I need and crack it open. Xyron approaches me with a smile on his face and a twinkle in his eye. A heart-warming greeting.

"Doing some research on magic I see? Anything I can help with?" Xyron questions.

"No," I lie, "I think I'm just nervous. I've spent all this time getting to Bagoa to talk to you and the other council members about our concerns. That now I'm finally here and it's surreal. I'm just trying to get rid of the anxiousness."

"Listen, you have nothing to worry about. There is only four other members. There's Quinn, he's pretty much our witch doctor and fine representative for the people of Bolyen. Second in line, we have Heavenly. She is a bit too serious at times but she means well. She's been through a lot she's pretty much in survivalist mode all the time."

"I know the feeling." I chime in.

"Third is Neelia, our female head of council. Our other witch doctor but she tends to act more as a voice of reason. Another way of putting it would be our tie breaker. When your apart of a council like this. Trust me you tend to need one." he laughs "Especially when Rain gets too serious and involved. Rain is the dragon you saw in the front room. He's the most serious person...or dragon you'll ever meet. But again means well. Finally there's me and I'm a Knight also known as the male head of council. So no worries."

"Thankyou." I say again "I really appreciate it."

"No problem. You look like you could have used some reassurance."

"Um...can I ask you something kinda personal," I say shyly.

"Sure anything." he says smiling, flashing his bright white teeth at me.

"Please don't take this the wrong way. But how did you become head of council?" I ask nervous and hesitantly.

A blank expression runs across his face. I have completely caught him off guard. He makes it seem as if there was no way of recovery from that question. No path to get back on, to resume a normal conversation.

"You don't have to answer if you don't want to!" I say immediately "I was just wondering. No just forget I even asked." I say turning away.

"No, it's fine. It's just no one's ever asked me that

before. The public didn't question it when I became head. They just went with it. I mean we've never had a problem with anyone in power before. So no worries, right?"

"So what happened?" I say gently.

"Well, nothing really. One day everything was fine. The council had let out like normal. Everything was normal. Everything was fine. But. . .we woke the next morning. All the members were called in for a meeting. What for, I don't know. But someone reported that my dad, Wilfred, never came. All the residents in the tower got worried so we searched for him. Eventually we found him. In his room. . . Still laying in his bed. Dead." Xyron tells me not allowing himself to get emotional about the whole thing.

"I'm so sorry." I state "I feel horrible."

"It's fine. The doctors concluded that he died of natural causes. He died quickly and more importantly peacefully. After that, I was appointed to be the male head of council. Mostly due to the fact I was his son and they didn't know who else to pick. Who would truly qualify and wouldn't be so far-fetched that it would throw the people of Xyron off. I grew up in the castle, so why not me."

"Wow."

"Not long after his death which was not announced to the public. I was appointed along with Neelia. A recommendation of some guy who works at a desk in the back named Finn. She only got in because she knew him and the council has this crazy rule of when you add one gender someone of the opposite gender must also be added. The rest is history."

"That's an interesting story," I say.

"Too bad nobody other than you and the other residents here will ever get a chance to hear it. Hey, I gotta go. But that book your holding is an interesting one. Long story short it tells you that if you were to know one thing about magic and nothing else. Know that magic starts with new discovered emotions and or accomplishments. It's a good read. Anyway, i'll see you tomorrow at the hearing."

"Alright, I think I'll head back to my room. I should get some sleep. Wouldn't want to be yawning and looking unprofessional while trying to present my concerns." I say right before he walks off.

"Yeah wouldn't want that." he laughs.

‡　　‡　　‡

Chapter 12

I take a long hot bath after I arrive at my extravagant room.
Open floor plans. Blood red bed sheets with the highest
thread count ever known on the circular beds. White throw
pillows everywhere. A window view, of course, looking over
Bagoa not that you could see it with it being night time.
Though it seems that there was a single lit torch somewhere
in a distance just glowing. Reminds me of a lighthouse just
not as bright.

Outside of that, I can't seem to get a certain thought
out of my head. I keep thinking of him. I just wanted to wash
my face with the hot but gentle towel. But as I ran over my
face I felt like I could feel his as well.
When I touched my ivory cheeks with hints of pink pigment
matched mines. It's not just because he smiled a lot but
because I don't know. I think I just see his happiness and joy.

His hopefulness and trying to remain strong reflecting my own. It was strange. It's weird.

It's like when you make a friend when your a child. You meet someone and your best friends minutes later. I feel like he's on my side. He's not just saying that to be kind. It's beyond that.

Not being able to rid my thoughts even with all my efforts to do so I decided to take a walk around the tower. I throw on a robe and try to think of what I'm going to say at my hearing tomorrow. Will they believe my concerns?

When I step out of my room, lock the door, and turn around I bump into someone. Looking up I see a woman with long black wavy hair, plump peach lips, and gold colored eyes to go with her olive skin. She was even more breath-taking than Mira.

"Sorry," I say.

"Don't worry about it? Um...I know this sounds weird but can we talk." she says to me.

"Of course," I say caught off guard "Your Neelia, the female head of council. Sure I'm flattered." I continue.

"Let's go to the official's balcony. We can talk and look at the stars there."

"Alright," I reply.

We head over to the balcony which has a view similar to the one to my room. Not much of a surprise considering the tower is round and my room is on the same side of this building. Being able to see more to the left though from our current standpoint I can see more of the blues and purples making up the galaxy. I can also see the tear drop planet Ivus glistening. Our sister planet. It's all just so nice. It'll be even better tomorrow.

"So what did you want to talk about?" I ask lightly.

"I'm not really sure. It was just nice to see another girl around. That's not on the council. One that's not so serious. I just want to relax. Though now that I think about it. What did bring you here?"

"To be honest I'm here purely on council matters. I wouldn't want to cause you more stress or anything. You just said you wanted to be less...council like." I say to her.

"Well, it's fine. It's the only thing I'm good at in my opinion. Shoot, tell me what you plan to tell the council tomorrow."

"Okay...if you insist. I want to tell the council that the Moxus injection is hurting our current day society. I'm worried that all the businesses will fail as well. Take no offense to this. But everything was going quite well before you two, you and Xyron, were put in very high positions of power. I just wanted to ask the council to revert back to the old ways. You know to put an end to the moxus injection."

"That sounds interesting."

She says grabbing at my throat and digging her nails into it. Lifting me off the ground I look at her. Neelia's eyes change to a light blue color. I reach for her hands in effort to pull them back.

What has gotten into her? It can't be what I said. That's not enough reason alone to kill a person. Plus I'm only asking the council. Which she's on. She can end it all when they vote on it. She doesn't need to choke me to death. The pain starts sinking in.

Neelia voice deepens, becoming a threatening tone of voice, less natural "Listen to me closely. Go home." she says "Go home and let this go. Don't get involved. It's a deadly game."

She drops me and I land on my feet and I gasp for air trying to fill my lungs. I try not to move my neck in fear of causing myself to create more pain.

She threatened me. . . I'm not sure if I want to run for my life. I feel like this might be more of a reason to go through with it. Maybe the guy back in La Bobo Cree was right. I do have a death wish.

"Hey guys, it's a bit late don't you think." Xyron calls out from the shadows "We all should be well rested for tomorrow. You can talk about girl stuff at a more reasonable time tomorrow." he laughs the last part.

"Your right." Neelia agrees "We should head in."

She throws me a charming smile and her eyes convert

back to their normal golden color. Did she hear him coming? I'm still touching some sensitive places on my neck checking for nail marks. Or bruising and maybe even blood.

I finally let myself fall over. Completely gasping for air. Letting my lungs fill all the way up. It feels like I'm gonna cough up blood sometimes I'm in so much pain. But I should be fine. It's a good thing Xyron showed up when he did.

‡   ‡   ‡

Chapter 13

I'm fully dressed, my hair is brushed, and there's nothing stuck in my teeth from breakfast. It's almost noon which means we are minutes from the hearing. I still haven't practiced what I'm going to say and there's no time to do it now.

All of last nights events are still lingering. After all I've done and all I've been through. From slavery and meeting Trixie to waking up this morning with the weight of Xyron on my shoulder. I can honestly say it was well worth it. If I was to die today by Neelia's hands. . .it'd all be worth it. I know I tried everything in my power.

I've relived the horrible events in my past. I escaped slavery and probably have a nice size bounty on my head. I somehow pissed off one of the leading members of the council. I survived the desert and the snow. Now, all I have to do is get through the speech. Open my mouth and let the words come out. Tell them my concerns and hope to persuade them to take action. Today is the moment of truth.

Today will be the time we find out if I am who I wanted to be all this time. A woman of confidence or a woman who hasn't progressed at all throughout this entire journey.

A clock strikes 12 somewhere in the building and rings throughout the tower and the town. Let the show begin. I head to the front room which doubles as the hearing room. It's convenient.

I arrive to see the 4 navy blue chairs each filled with a member of the council. I stand in the center of the room. From left to right there is Heavenly, dark chocolate skin with golden blonde hair and light blue eyes. Tribal paint on her face. She really is in survivalist mode all the time but she's on the more, extremist end of it. Her face neutral. Dare I even say bored.

Next to Heavenly is Quinn, tall with an ivory skin tone, red hair, and brown eyes. He's normal looking. Seemingly human. Not sure how he can represent the people of Bolyen accurately given the following. He's not a spirit of the underwater city. But the council makes the calls. They know more than I do.

After that is Xyron who right now I will fully admit

he is definitely my favorite. Always busy and stays upbeat not to mention he doesn't threaten me in the middle of the night. Speaking of threats the lovely lady beside him is Neelia the innocent.

Though I now hate her guts and know she's actually crazy I will maintain a smile and pretend it didn't happen. She's still on the council but I have 4 other members I need to convince right now. There are more important matters. That's getting my point across.

Finally there is Rain our lovely security system and everyone's favorite dragon. Hopefully he'll remain calm and not stomp on me with his big dragon claws. He can be reasonable I'm sure.

Xyron stands up his purple cape flowing "Alright if everyone is ready. Let us commence the hearing. Audrey, you may begin." he smiles as he sits back down into his seat.

Oh great, they are all officially staring at me. Engaged. Listening to my every word. Audrey, you haven't said anything yet. Speak! Speak! My brain yells at me. Don't screw this is up at the last second. You can do this. You need to do this now. Speak now or forever hold your peace. Do you understand me?

"Okay, so my first and most important concern. The moxus injection. When this was announced to the public it was seen as a potentially good idea. It was a new mean for

113

businesses to open and make money. After all the moxus injection does cost a few Alfies to get. Knowing that getting the moxus injection would kill you is one thing. But I do think that it has had many unintended consequences. I think the only one that was taken into account when the council made this decision was the birth and death rate. But there is more to it than that. Which is why my other concern is the business owners themselves." I start off.

"The business owners are fine." Neelia tries to write it off.

"No, actually they're not." I state not letting myself get agitated with her remark "Have you traveled the regions lately. On my voyage here to talk to you I passed through the Northern Trisector. It looks worst than it did DURING the Trogonese war. That's saying something. Beggars have multiplied beyond belief. No one is safe. Everywhere I traveled I saw lines out the door for the Moxus injection. I couldn't watch it was so heartbreaking to see. The creatures in the line where business owners. After the council removed some of the funding from business owners they couldn't keep their businesses open. They couldn't support their families. So the main creatures and inhabitants in these lines are old business owners. Who not only get the moxus injection for themselves but their children. Usually from ages around seven and younger."

Shock runs across different members faces. I swear I could

hear Xyron's heartbreak from prior words. Anything with a heart would feel awful knowing that they contributed to that. Or just hear that it was happening. So, of course, Neelia's face didn't change at all. I swear she's not even human.

"How tragic." Heavenly lets out.
"I myself am a follower of the Alfralon religion. We believe in respecting other religions. This is a good thing. I follow this belief to a T. But I must admit that I did have another experience on my travel here. I met a girl, Trixie, as you might have ran into her this morning I'm sure."

The council laughs at this.
"She," I begin "was a slave when I met her. To a Poldano named Tocra. Trixie ended up in slavery because of her mothers array of problems. She lost Trixie while gambling leaving that poor girl in slavery. Being exposed to things she shouldn't have seen. She probably did things she shouldn't have had to participate in."

The councils face show me that they are reflecting on the decision. Letting it weigh on their minds. Saying was this for the best? Could we have made a mistake? Which means they are listening they might actually make a change.
I continue " I understand that the council can not change the beliefs of religions. Or the ideals of religion itself. But can the council put some parameters on the matter? For instance can

they make it so that only people of a certain age like 16 can only be brought in under the Belanox slavery belief. Leaving the young and innocence ones who are still learning the works of life out of it. That way they are not affected like Trixie was. I mean Trixie was in slavery majority of her life."

"What does that last part have to do with anything?" Neelia questions.

"Everyone has been affected for the worst by some of your most recent rulings. I want the council to consider that it might not have turned out the way it was planned. The council is supposed to help the people. Represent the people. Currently it's not doing that." I say trying to hold back the accusatory tone.

"The people of Xyron will be fine," Neelia says sternly.

"Have you been out there lately. Have you seen it with your own eyes?" I look at each member of the council "I have." I add "I've seen it. I lived it. I breathed it." I look at Neelia again "You guys make your decision from inside the tower with little contact of the outside world recently. Which is why I came here. Inside the tower. Trixie and I are living breathing proof that it's not easy out there. Not easy the way you think it is."

"Why don't more people come to complain then?" she shoots back.

"Because they're to busy trying to survive. Protect their family. Run their businesses. I don't have a family anymore. I was raised by grandfather in the earlier years of my life and he fed me to the wolves and left me. I was raised to fend for myself. Not to get involved with others too much. He taught me to be nomadic and never to settle down. These issues and consequences are affecting the people who have settled down with their spouse and kids. They need to worry about putting food on the table for five. I only have me and recently Trixie. Lennox also fends for herself to my knowledge."

"Then wh-" Neelia starts.

"Enough!" Xyron stops us jumping out of his seat.

Silence falls upon the room. Everyone looking at him hardly blinking. Barely breathing. Suddenly I notice that I'm sweating a bit and everything feels a bit hot. Did me and Neelia really allow ourselves to get so worked up? That isn't known to happen in a formal hearing. The air is thick and heavy. We're all frozen waiting on the next social cue. Xyron adjusts his shirt "Excuse my outburst. I think we've all heard enough to make a decision. Maybe we've all had enough time to think of our own counter arguments and or resolutions to the problems Audrey has pointed out here. So I hereby end this hearing. The Council will break for lunch." he looks at his watch "It's now one p.m. So we'll take an hour break. The council will eat and meet back here at two. Discuss things and come to a conclusion. Audrey" he looks at me "You should know the results of your hearing at 3." He then leaves the room in what is seemingly an aggravated matter.

When he storms out of the hearing room everyone kinda just stares at each other. Looking for some confirmation in this surreal moment. Can he just end a hearing like that? After we all finish awkwardly moving around and staring we all take the recommended break. Everyone either heads to their rooms or the dining hall. I stand in place moments after everyone has left. Staring at the ceiling wondering what have I done.

Trixie skips up next to me "So how'd your hearing go?"

‡   ‡   ‡

Chapter 14

"The hearing was interesting," I say to Trixie who now sits beside me in the dining hall.

"So it did go well." She says smiling while popping one bright red strawberry after another in her mouth.

"Not exactly," I state as I pick at the bread flaking off of my croissant.

"Did you say everything you wanted to say?" she asks.

"I think so."

"So, if you said everything you wanted to say. You did what you said you were gonna do. How did things not go well? It sounds like a mission accomplished to me. You should be happy. Enjoy the food here."

"Alright, I will," I say giving in.

"Yes, finally, Let's eat like royalty. You'll be the queen and I'll be the princess." she states.

We walk back over to the tables of food. I actually fill up my plate this time. Now it won't be so lonely with the single croissant I was picking at earlier. Trixie's right I should enjoy it while it last. We can't live in the tower forever.

I never even thought of what I'd do after this. What does one do after doing something like this? Do I just go back home? Where ever home is. In my case. . .the adventure is over and I just walk from here. Me, my staff on my left, and the clothes on my back.
I might help Trixie get all the way back to Bolyen so she can be with her mother once again. If that's what she wants. But even if that were to happen. The question still remains. What about after that.

When one chapter of your life closes and comes to an end, a new chapter opens and a new adventure begins. So where to life? Am I just suppose to pick a path and follow it and see what happens next?
I can't do that. What if I do that and end up in La Bobo Cree. Or worst Eil Poldane. There's definitely a bounty on my head by now. If someone did find me they might just collect the bounty. Other times they collect the rewards and then shoot the bounty. Who knows what will happen to me when I leave here.

"Trixie, I'm sorry I just can't eat right now. I'm too anxious. I'm gonna take a walk around the tower. I'll meet you back here and we can walk to the hearing room together to get the results."

"Fine." she says "I'll eat like a queen without you then. No bagels with cream cheese or blueberry muffins for you."

I walk away. Aimlessly wandering the halls. It's like I'm looking to run into trouble. But everywhere I look there seems to be trouble. I walk pass numerous doors they all look exactly the same. How have I managed to not get lost yet? Or dizzy for that matter. That's when I hear something strange.

"So, what happened?" a male voice says.

"The council seems to be considering her claims." Neelia says.

"NO! We can't have this happen. We are too close to our goal now." the male voice yells.

"What should I do then?" she asks.

I peer around the corner quickly to see a male standing up. He has a light complexion and wears boxy black glasses. His hair curly and a brownish color that stops at his ears. Shaved facial hair. Other than that he was a typical nerd at the glance of things.

"You're an AI system created by me, Finn. Do whatever is necessary. Convince them that we shouldn't change anything. Not for any reason. Remind them that she's some peasant girl. She doesn't know anything about being in a position of authority. How could she know what's best for the people. The council has more important things to do."

Why does that name sound familiar. Finn, Finn, Finn. OH! Finn, Xyron was mentioning him when he was telling me about how no one else outside of this tower would ever know how his father died. Finn is just an ordinary guy that works here. At least that's the impression he gave everyone else.

"This girl." Finn states "Is sticking her nose where it doesn't belong. Do you understand that Neelia! We could lose it all. Please get her out of here." he says in a more sad desperate voice "If you get her out of here. We'll be that much closer to ruling all of Xyron. Just you and me. I'll be the king and you'd be my loving and faithful bride. No one, I mean no one, will ever look down on the Gaulden's again." Did he just propose to an Artificial Intelligence system? So Neelia isn't human after all. There's more to Finn than everyone thinks. How will I warn them? What should I do?

The clock rings at the hour. Time to head to the dining hall to meet Trixie. As the bell rings, I take off running. They won't be able to hear my footsteps as I take off. Wouldn't want them to know I was eavesdropping on them. Neelia almost took my life once. I don't want her to give her a reason to succeed.

‡   ‡   ‡

Chapter 15

Arriving at the dining room I see Lennox and Trixie waiting for me. I'm still trying to gather my thoughts from all of what I've heard. Things just keep getting more and more serious. We all stand together. Take a deep breath. I think I'm more nervous than anyone in this entire building.

Trixie looks at me "Everything will turn out great, Audrey. Don't worry." she states.

A Guardsman walks into the dining hall with armor on. Is that really necessary I think to myself. Why have guards now at the result phase and not the actual hearing? Did someone not like their results in past hearings? Who knows cause I refuse to ask. I'm afraid of the answer I might get.

We all head over to the hearing room the automatic doors open before us. You can hear the air pressure. I'm on edge now looking at all the council members again. Did it get cold in here or what? Everything seems so serious and formal. Even more so than before. Am I suppose to say something? No just stand here I tell myself.

Xyron rises from his chair his purple cape flowing once again. He walks towards me and stands towards my right. Lennox and Trixie to the left of me. My heart is banging against my rib cage. My ears are throbbing. My throat is becoming dry. I hold my breath I'm so nervous. Breathe I remind myself. You really need to calm down.

"I, Xyron, Male lead of the council. Hereby state that in favor o-"

Xyron falls to the ground abruptly with a silent crash. Or maybe it wasn't silent. I just didn't hear it because all I can hear was my heart breaking inside of me. My hands touching my face in shock. The world around me had slowed down right before my very eyes. I wanted to cry and scream. But instead I look to my left to see the shooter. Neelia.

There she stands at her seat tall with her head high and gyan bolter in hand. A weapon that shoots deadly magic. I look back down at Xyron as he grips at his chest. I see his blood pouring out of him and onto his hand. He's choking. He can't breathe. The black acidic magic is eating away at him. I want to help him.

"Audrey, Audrey," I hear "Audrey!" screams Trixie.

The world speeds back up. A fight has broken out in

the room. All the guardsman and members of the council. Even Lennox and Trixie and they weren't even all that involved. Everyone is at each other's throats. Blood is being shed like there's no tomorrow. I even find that while I was in shock blood has even splattered onto my own clothes. Blood drawn by spears, knives, and even swords.

"Audrey! It's now or never. Do what you gotta do. Hurry!"

I run towards the elevator unscathed. Get me out of this chaos. This is more than I signed up for. People are dying and fighting. I didn't ask for this. I just wanted to help make things better I cry on the inside. I just wanted to make things right again. Yet people are still dying. Can nothing make the madness stop. Alfralon gods where are you now? I need you. Save me, Save us. Stop the acts of murder and bloodshed.

"I can't handle this!" I scream in agony when I deem myself safe in the elevator.

Recalling what Mira said about having to do this on my own. I had to do this without the gods. Without any help at all. I was the only one who could help. The only one who could save us.

"Why couldn't this staff have found someone else. Why me?!" I yell completely self-destructing.

I wipe my tears from my face. Are you crazy? This is no time for tears. You better go do what you came here to do. You escaped slavery. You saved a little girl's life. You finally made it to Bagoa. There is a war right outside this elevator. That your friends are fighting in. It is way too late to back out now. My left hand tightens around the staff. Get it together and finish this.

I take my right hand and hit the button with the Crossed out B. I'm guessing it'll take me to my destination. The area that's off limits. . .the basement. It gives the appearance of not working but something tells me it does.

‡   ‡   ‡

Chapter 16

The elevator stops with a loud thud. The doors begin to
creak apart. When I step out I see him standing there staring
at me. He stares me down and I don't make a sound. It's just
us two and the sigil engraved in the ground in gold behind
him. It's like I'm walking on eggshells.

"Move out of the way," I say.

"Sorry I can't do that." he says.

"Why not? It's for the good of Xyron? Wait it works!?"
I say a bit shocked.

Him being down here is actual proof that it works. If it
didn't there would be no reason for him to guard it. If it
didn't work no one would need to be down here. This floor
wouldn't even need to exist. But it does. And he is here
trying to stop me.

"Of course it works." Finn says "You came down here
not knowing if it works or not?" he says.

"I came here to find out if the myths are true," I state.

"Well, I'm here to tell you. The sigil works. However, I can't let you activate it."

"Which brings us back to why not?"

"BECAUSE," Finn says getting aggravated " The Gaulden family has been protecting the sigil for generations. In secrecy generation after generation. Never getting a speck of credit. Your famous council members. Some of them don't even know my name despite how important my job is. I'm just some guy that also lives in the tower with them."

I try to walk slowly to get around him as he talks but he catches me and I freeze in my tracks.

"I CAN'T LET YOU ACTIVATE IT!" he screams crazily "My cousin Guinevere died keeping this sigil inactive since Neelia and Xyron got appointed. This is how things are suppose to be. This is what Xyron is. This is its true form and members of society."

"What do you mean?" I ask.

"When the sigil is activated it sends out a magical pulse throughout the planet. This pulse brainwashes every single inhabitant into doing their best. Only being the purely good side of themselves. It takes away their free will. Their ability to make their own decisions. They can only feel happy on the inside."

"Is that such a bad thing?" I point out.

"PEOPLE NEED PAIN!" Finn shouts "They need to cry and make bad decisions and learn from their mistakes. They need to be themselves no matter how ugly they might be. That's how things are suppose to work. You can't just live peacefully forever."

"So you have no intentions of activating it."

"Of course I do. I will be the one to activate the sigil when Xyron has reached it's lowest point. When it has completely hit rock bottom. Then I, Finn Gaulden, will activate it by myself. Giving the Gaulden name honor. Then my family. . .my race will get the attention we deserve. We aren't just servants for you people to boss around and treat like some errand boy. We are people. We deserve respect." he explains.

He's hurt. He is breaking down on the inside. He just wants to get what he thinks his people deserve. Finn thinks he's doing the right thing for his people and his family. Finn also has something to prove. Even if all of Xyron ends up dying. I pity him. What he went through in his past and what he continues to go through right now. It must be a terrible pain to bare all by yourself. Especially with his cousin Guinevere's death.

"Sorry, Finn. But I didn't come here to fail." I say as I dash pass him with my staff.

I've caught him off guard. I'm not really sure what to do next or how to activate the sigil in this environment but I'll have to figure it out. *Clank.* What is he doing? Did he just try to hit me with a pipe?!?! I stop in my tracks to turn around and use my staff to block his attacks.

Why does he hit so hard? I thought he sat behind a desk all day. Where did all this strength come from? *Clank, Clink, Clank.* The staff and pipe collide against each other swing after swing. He brings down the pipe harder each time. Sparks begin to fly due to the clashing metals. "I don't have time for this!" I say as I push him back with my staff.

Finn falls back onto the sigil landing on his back. I look around frantically trying to come up with my next move. I'm running out of time. I don't have time to fight him. Trixie and Lennox are still upstairs fighting off the others. I hope they're still alive. Come on Audrey make a move. I take my well-weighted staff and grip it firmly. I bash a nearby pipe. Hopefully, whatever is in it will create a barrier between us. It will buy me more time. When I pull the staff back out water starts spewing everywhere.

‡   ‡   ‡

Chapter 17

"NO!" Finn screams.

The water has filled the last bit of the sigil. Every single area of the magical sigil is sealed. The world stops and is completely still. First, there is nothing. No sound, heartbeat, movement. I don't think my thoughts exist either. This is just the aftermath of my brain processing. A ringing sound then fills the air. Like a really loud plop of one single drop of water falling into the ocean. When the ripple is all yet faded normalcy returns.

"Did it work?" I say aloud now being able to speak "That's all?" I say a bit confused.
I look down and panic. Finding myself standing in water up to my waist. How long were we all frozen in time? How long was that sound really? How much water was that pipe releasing? I have to get out of here. I must go and check on the others. Wait! Where is Finn?

I search the waters around me quickly looking in every direction. Come on where is he. I soon spot his body motionless, floating, and possibly dead. I trudge through the high waters to get to him.

I yank his body out of the water by his shirt. His curly brown hair dripping wet. I continue to hold him. His head pointed downward. He coughs up water. His body starts to move as well.

"NO, LET ME DIE! I HAVE NOTHING TO LIVE FOR! I FAILED!" he shouts in angry sorrows.

"We all have something to live for," I say still holding him by the collar.

"I FAILED YOU GUINEVERE! I'M SORRY." he weeps ignoring my statement.

"LISTEN! Whether you failed or not. You're not getting out of this by drowning yourself. Suicide isn't the answer."

"BUT I DESERVE DEATH." he spits at me in a dark and almost demonic tone.

Man, this guy is delusional and messed up in the head. First, he wants to marry the Artificial Intelligence system. Then he tries to kill himself. He's all over the place. I need to take him to the council. Hopefully, they'll know what to do with him.

I drag Finn to the elevator with me and we take it back to where the party is. When I step out of the elevator the only thing I see is Trixie using magic. A dragon made of white energy wrapped around her. Which she then uses to wipe out Neelia. The dragon flows straight through Neelia's body and she short circuits. She falls to her knees and then her face hits the floor. Everyone else seems to be dead.

‡   ‡   ‡

Chapter 18

I step out the elevator and into the front room dragging Finn with me. I analyze the room carefully and slowly. All the windows are blown out and shattered. Blood and dead bodies decorate are newly colored floor. Dark red everywhere. They all wear some type of war paint on their clothes. No way to tell if its blood that has been shed by others. Or they are wearing some of their own. The once leather seats are now scratched beyond recognition really. They also bleed out their insides. Nothing in this room went untouched.

"How did this happen. I mean did having a dragon here even help." I say in horror.
Quinn answers "Yeah, he kept his cool and didn't turn us all to bar-be-que. He made a wonderful shield. However, our other members didn't seem to want to be on the defensive

side of this chaos."

Quinn approaches Lennox who seems to be unaffected by the prior events that have played out in front of her. Her face still and blank. As if she had become bored all over again now that the moment of chaos had passed. I swear for someone who seemed to be running away when we first met. She truly seems to be a thrill seeker underneath it all.

"Alright. The chaos is over. Once again things seem to have come back to you. You are the only one left once again. Now that the boy is dead. May his soul rest in peace."

When Quinn says that I remember that Xyron had been shot. I run to his side and hold his already cold body in my arms. His lips have also lost the pink pigment they once held. This can't be. He's too nice and innocent. He doesn't deserve this.

"No, No, he can't be. Wake up!" I yell lightly shaking his lifeless body.

My eyes tear up, and it's not long after that my face is completely covered by my own tears. My heart beat slows. I can't make out my thoughts or feelings. I don't know why I feel the way I do. Even if I did meet him yesterday. He was the nicest person that I'd met on this journey. Every time I saw him he had a smile. He was even helpful. Even outside of saving my life last night when Neelia was choking me.

"WAKE UP!"

"He's dead. Let it go." says Lennox in a cold and heartless tone "And to answer your question, Quinn. No, I'm not joining the council. Or forming a new one. Or any other type of authority role over Xyron."

"You have to. You are the only qualified one left to fill the position."

"You and Rain would manage just fine."

"We can't. The meeting we had before today we had officially retired and given up our seats. We were here today only for looks. I'm sure as you can see we didn't think everyone else would die. The council is dead and we have no authority now. You're the next rightful person in line. And must I emphasize this again. The ONLY QUALIFIED PERSON."

"Not true." Lennox says.

I don't know why this is playing out so strangely. I have no idea what's going on. Why is Quinn talking to Lennox? How do they know each other? How is Lennox of all people qualified to run this planet? What has the world come to?

I don't know. But it's true whether Lennox likes it or not. Someone has to be in a position of power. Old council members have to retire after a certain period of time and they aren't allowed back onto the council. Even in a situation like this. Granted, a situation like this has never occurred. So there aren't really any firm rules on this situation. But there are no official council member to make the call. No one to make a new law.

"The girl can do it. SHE is the daughter, the last child of the Wakaun line." says Lennox.

She then turns into a blinding bright white light. We all turn our heads and look away. I have the suspicion if I even tried to continue to look in her direction that I'd go blind. The light becomes a soft glow. It's safe to look again. "Grandpa?!" I say in confusion.

"Yes, it's me. Audrey is next in line now that her FRATERNAL TWIN BROTHER is now dead." my grandfather says with a smile "Don't tell me you two didn't see the resemblance."

Everyone in the room just stares at my grandfather without a word. No one dares to second-guess what he's saying. We all just listen.

"You see." he continues "When both of your parents were still alive Audrey. After your mother had given birth to you both. Your parents got into a fight. Your father Wilfred soon to be male lead of the council wanted to raise you both in the tower. As if you were both royalty. Giving you everything you deserved in life. Your mother though had the fear that being raised in the tower would spoil you too much. Probably isolate you from not being able to relate to the other children throughout Xyron. Again your father thought you'd be fine, you'd be safe. Though to very recent events, we know that no longer stands true because Xyron is dead. Anyway eventually their argument was blown out of proportion. They decided to get a divorce."

I can't help but think that this is all a little too good to be true. I can't tell if my grandfather is lying to get out of this. Or actually telling the truth. I'm confused. I looked up to him as a kid. He always did what was right. But he still is a lazy drunkard. Even if he was Lennox when he was drunk.

"Your mother took you, Audrey. Your dad took your brother Xyron. In all the back and forth bickering there was one thing, they could ultimately agree on. Only a woman could raise a woman. A man could raise a man. They parted ways taking a twin with them. In the end, they both died of natural causes. Xyron was apparently continued to be raised by the other members of the remaining council. Your mother died of an unknown sickness and put you in my care. The rest was history."

"WHY WASN'T I TOLD ABOUT ANY OF THIS!" Quinn says in a shocked and angry tone of voice "Excuse my sudden outburst." he says calming himself.

"You weren't on the council yet." my grandpa points out "As you mentioned before. We definitely didn't think one day all of the council members would all wake up and get slaughtered on the same day."

"Fine. . .very well then." Quinn turns to me "Are you interested in becoming queen or new head council of all of Xyron?"

‡　　‡　　‡

Chapter 19

I look down at my brothers cold and dead body. Looking
and searching for the answers in his eyes. As if he'd come
back alive even for a second to choke out the answer of what
I should do. Tell me Xyron. What would you have done? I
don't know if I have what it takes.

You look like you could have used some reassurance. I
remember him saying to me.
I continue to hold him waiting for an answer. A sign of sorts.
Anything. Like I said I just wanted to make things right.
Becoming ruler of an entire planet was not one. But is this
my next step? I did wonder not long ago what I should do
after this. It seems there's only one thing to do.

"Yes," I say with authority in my voice "I, Audrey,
will take my brother Xyron's place on the throne. I will
restore Xyron back to the peaceful and loving country it once
was. The way I remember it."

"Okay great. Now that you all got that settled. What are you going to do with me? I am still here you know." Finn complains still on his knees like some slave dripping wet with water.

Quinn raises an eyebrow at me. Acknowledging that there is no better time than the present to start acting like a person of higher authority. I nod at him accepting my first task as queen. I leave Xyron's dead body and walk over to Finn. I hover over him like a tower. He just looks up at me from the ground. No remorse in his eyes. He even dares to wear a smirk on his face.

Right now I hold all the power. I hold his life in my hands. I'm not sure what to make of the situation I'm so angry. He has caused bloodshed, sorrow, and tried to off himself. I'm not sure what he wants. What he loves. Not even what the delusional man in front of me who is on his knees fears. Cause it is certainly not me.

"The crimes you committed are punishable by death." I state.

He looks up at me with a demonic smile.

I squat down to get on eye level "But I won't do that. You're not taking the easy way out." I whisper "You are going to live with the fact that you failed. You're going to live knowing that you aren't ruling this planet. You aren't married to Neelia and you never will be even if you manage to repair her because I forbid it."

"What!" he shouts going into a rage.

The smile drops to his face. He has a crazy look in his eye. I stand up and back away.

Trixie uses her energy dragon to restrain him. She wraps her dragon around him like a Boa constrictor. It squeezes him tighter every time he struggles.

"Calm yourself." says Trixie.

"I'm keeping a close eye on you, Finn. You're not going anywhere." I finish.

"Alright. On that note, I'm out of here. You seem to have everything under control. Audrey, your welcome. You have a throne beneath your feet that is all yours." he shoots a look at Quinn "Which means I'm off the hook. I can continue to drink myself into a coma." he says getting into the elevator.

Quinn and I watch him leave. Trixie keeping an eye on Finn.

"By the way Audrey. Now that you know it's me and everything. I want you to know the truth about your childhood. The part you shared with me. I knew *everything* that was happening to you. . .I just didn't do anything about it." he states nonchalantly.

The elevator door shuts with a loud thud. I'm not really sure how to feel about the words that echo throughout my mind now. Is it worth mourning over after all these years? He knew all this time. But it's the past and we can't change the past. I have power over all of Xyron. I sculpt the future from now on.

Even if I wanted to chase him down or place a bounty on his head later. What purpose would it serve? He raised me as a survivalist. I went years without seeing him. If I can't find him no one can. So when the doors closed just now. I'm sure that was my last time seeing him for another 10 years or so. If not the rest of my lifetime.

Quinn looks at me.

Chapter 20

Standing on the balcony in my white dress with a lace veil covering my face feels strange. Not only because the dress seems more appropriate for a wedding. It's more because today is the day of my coronation. Which means the journey is over. It means I'm standing on the balcony of where my life was once threatened. It means I can clear the bounty on Trixie's head and myself. I can change many things.

When I began this journey I thought it was going to be me traveling alone. Doing the impossible. I truly didn't believe I would make it this far. Not to mention the outcome is completely different. On this journey I found myself. I surpassed my goals which I thought were way beyond my reach. I went through many obstacles in between. Now that I'm about to be crowned queen I'm sure there is many more to come. But I guess that's another journey in itself.

Quinn starts the ceremonial speech. I stand behind the special curtains that he put in place. It's bright outside. The sun shining brightly and melting the snow in Bagoa. I can imagine thousands of people below us waiting for the announcement. They don't know what they're going to hear. They don't know that I'm being crowned queen. They just know that all creatures and inhabitants were to come to the ceremonial square. And if they did they got the day off work. I rid my thoughts and listen to Quinn speak.

"Gather around everyone. I have good news and I have bad news. The bad news is that the council members have chosen to retire. We've decided that it is for the best. We've lost our vision of the future and we've lost our values in what's important to us. Whose important to us. But please, do not worry. Do not be sad. Do not mourn you're lost for the beloved council members. We leave you in good hands." Quinn tells the townspeople.
I take a deep breath. My hands begin to tremble.

"I present to you your new queen." he states.
I step through the curtains so the townspeople can see me in my beautiful white dress. All of it's embroideries and sigils. With every stitch of historical events embedded in it. They can see every pearl sparkle and all the gold shine. I can feel all the eyes below shifting their view to me.

"The last child in the Wakaun line, Audrey." Quinn

says as he flips my veil back revealing how I look to the public.

"A true visionary. Someone who has fought for and kept Xyron's best interest in mind when even the council was lost and unsure. She promises to continue to love and cherish Xyron and lead it back to it's peaceful state. With that being said." Quinn smiles "What will you do next?"

"I will …

‡   ‡   ‡

About The Author

Oops! She accidentally became an author. Erin started off as a normal psychology major. Then one day she randomly decided to sit down and write her very first book. Between being in love with authors, wanting to be self-employed, discovering self-publishing, and wanting to share her creativity. She dived straight in.

To get started she took Neil Gaiman's quote to heart. "This is how you do it: you sit down at the keyboard and you put one word after another until its done. It's that easy, and that hard." So she did exactly that. Next thing she knew her very first book was born. Yes, this book your holding in your very own hands. Once she finished she decided to publish it for all the world to see.
After all, there was nothing stopping her.

Visit her at:
thewritersscene.com
facebook.com/ohsweetmomsen
twitter.com/ohsweetmomsen
Instagram: @OhSweetMomsenAuthor